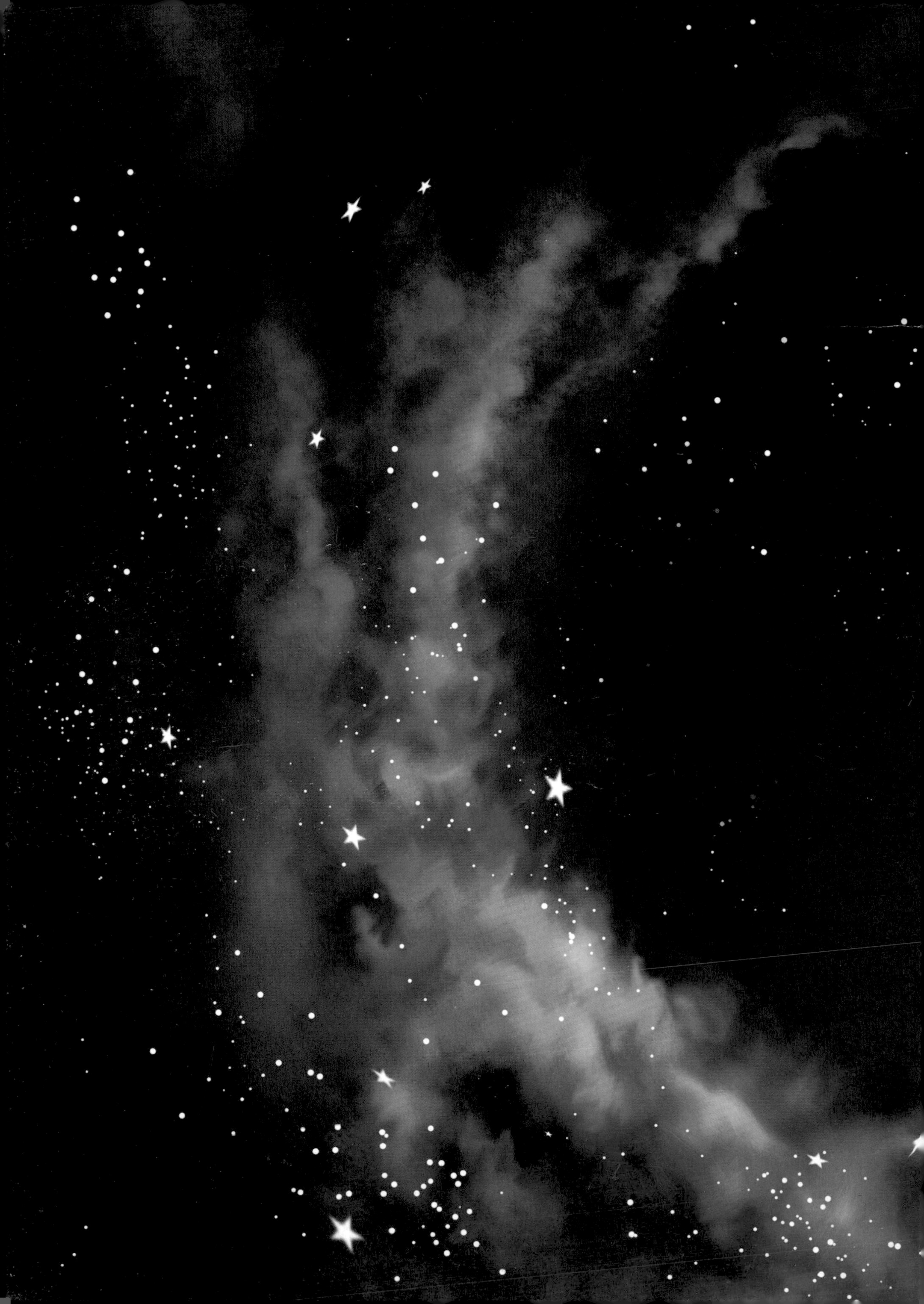

My dear Rose,

I learned a lot about our relationship with nature during our adventure on the Planet of the Giant.

An environment and its inhabitants develop together, and the people must never forget to live in harmony with their homeland, protecting and caring for it.

The Snake rejects this wise view because he seeks to destroy every planet.

More than ever, Fox and I dedicate ourselves to protecting all the inhabitants of the universe—as well as the worlds that sustain them!

The Little Prince

First American edition published in 2013 by Graphic Universe™.

Le Petit Prince ™

based on the masterpiece by Antoine de Saint-Exupéry

© 2013 LPPM
An animated series based on the novel *Le Petit Prince* by Antoine de Saint-Exupéry
Developed for television by Matthieu Delaporte, Alexandre de la Patellière, and Bertrand Gatignol
Directed by Pierre-Alain Chartier

© 2013 ÉDITIONS GLÉNAT
Copyright © 2013 by Lerner Publishing Group, Inc., for the current edition

Graphic Universe™ is a trademark of Lerner Publishing Group, Inc.

Graphic Universe™
A division of Lerner Publishing Group, Inc.
241 First Avenue North
Minneapolis, MN 55401 U.S.A.

Website address : www.lernerbooks.com

Library of Congress Cataloging-in-Publication Data

Dorison, Guillaume.
  [Planète des Wagonautes. English]
  The planet of Trainiacs / story by Anne-Claire N'Leh ; design and illustrations by Elyum Studio ; adapted by Guillaume Dorison ; translation, Anne Collins Smith and Owen Smith. — 1st American ed.
    p.   cm. — (The little prince ; #10)
  ISBN 978-0-7613-8760-2 (lib. bdg. : alk. paper)
  ISBN 978-1-4677-1653-6 (eBook)
  1. Graphic novels. I. Smith, Anne Collins, translator. II. Smith, Owen (Owen M.), translator. III. N'Leh, Anne-Claire. IV. Saint-Exupéry, Antoine de, 1900-1944. Petit Prince. V. Elyum Studio. VI. Petit Prince (Television program) VII. Title.
  PZ7.7.B8Po 2013
  741.5'944—dc23   2013000320

Manufactured in the United States of America
1 — DP — 7/15/13

THE NEW ADVENTURES
BASED ON THE MASTERPIECE BY ANTOINE DE SAINT-EXUPÉRY

The Little Prince

THE PLANET OF TRAINIACS

Based on the animated series and an original story by Anne-Claire N'Leh

Design: Elyum Studio
Story: Guillaume Dorison
Artistic Direction: Didier Poli
Art: Christine Chatal
Backgrounds: Isa Python
Coloring: Gwenaëlle Daligault
Editing: Christine Chatal
Editorial Consultant: Didier Convard

Translation: Anne and Owen Smith

Graphic Universe™ • Minneapolis

★ THE LITTLE PRINCE

The Little Prince has extraordinary gifts. His sense of wonder allows him to discover what no one else can see. The Little Prince can communicate with all the beings in the universe, even the animals and plants. His powers grow over the course of his adventures.

The Prince's uniform:
When he transforms into the uniform of a prince, he is more agile and quick. When faced with difficult situations, the Little Prince also uses a sword that lets him sketch and bring to life anything from his imagination.

His sketchbook:
When he is not in his Prince's clothing, the Little Prince carries a sketchbook. When he blows on the pages, they take wing and form objects that he'll find very useful. Like his sword, it's powered by stardust collected on his travels.

★ FOX

A grouch, a trickster, and, so he says, interested only in his next meal, Fox is in reality the Little Prince's best friend. As such, he is always there to give him help but also just as much to help him to grow and to learn about the world.

★ THE SNAKE

Even though the Little Prince still does not know exactly why, there can be no doubt that the Snake has set his mind to plunging the entire universe into darkness! And to accomplish his goal, this malicious being is ready to use any form of deception. However, the Snake never takes action himself. He prefers to bring out the wickedness in those beings he has chosen to bite, tempting them to put their own worlds in danger.

★ THE GLOOMIES

When people who have been "bitten" by the Snake have completely destroyed their own planets, they become Gloomies, slaves to their Snake master. The Gloomies act as a group and carry out the Snake's most vile orders so he can get the better of the Little Prince!

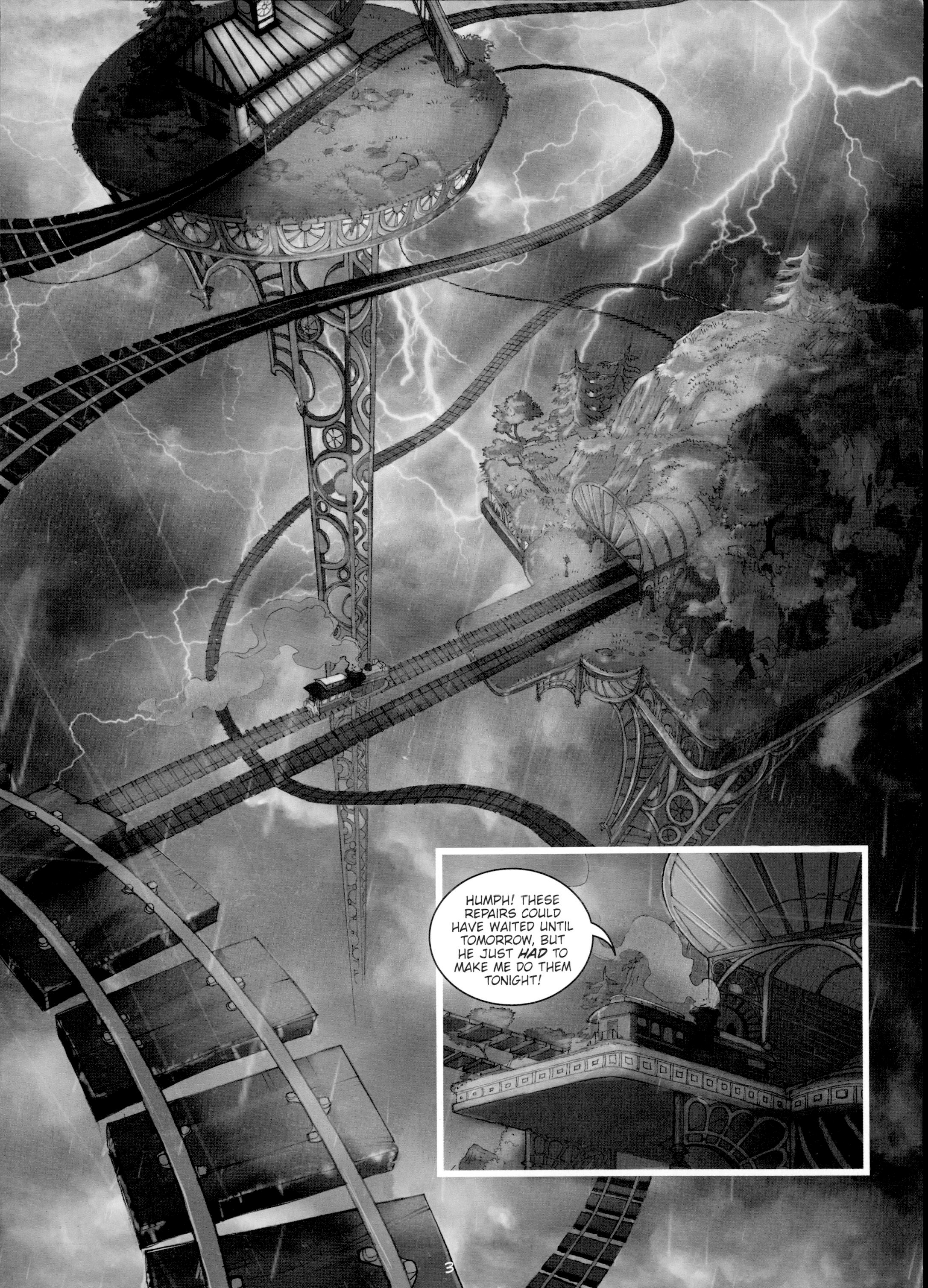
HUMPH! THESE REPAIRS COULD HAVE WAITED UNTIL TOMORROW, BUT HE JUST HAD TO MAKE ME DO THEM TONIGHT!

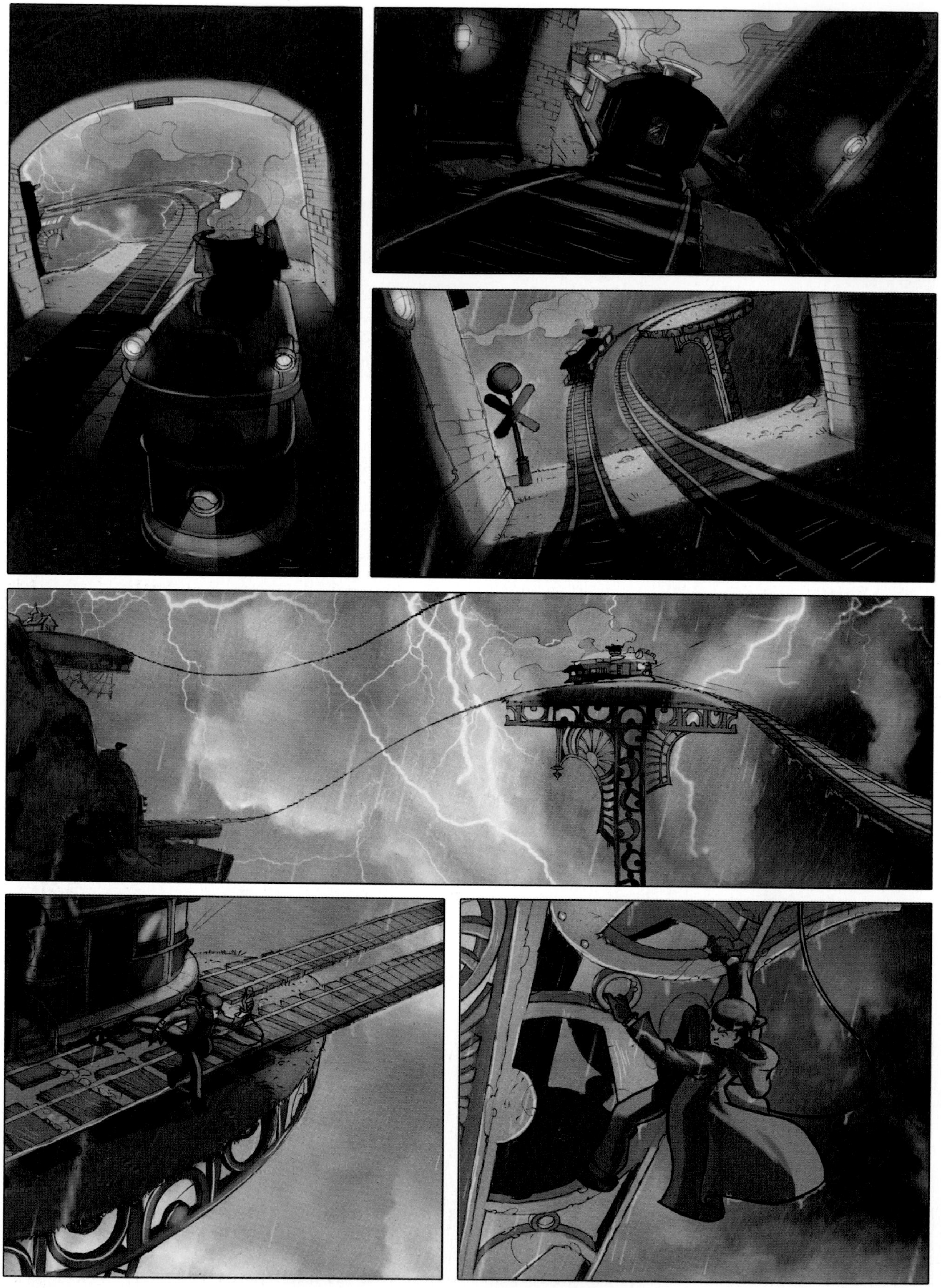

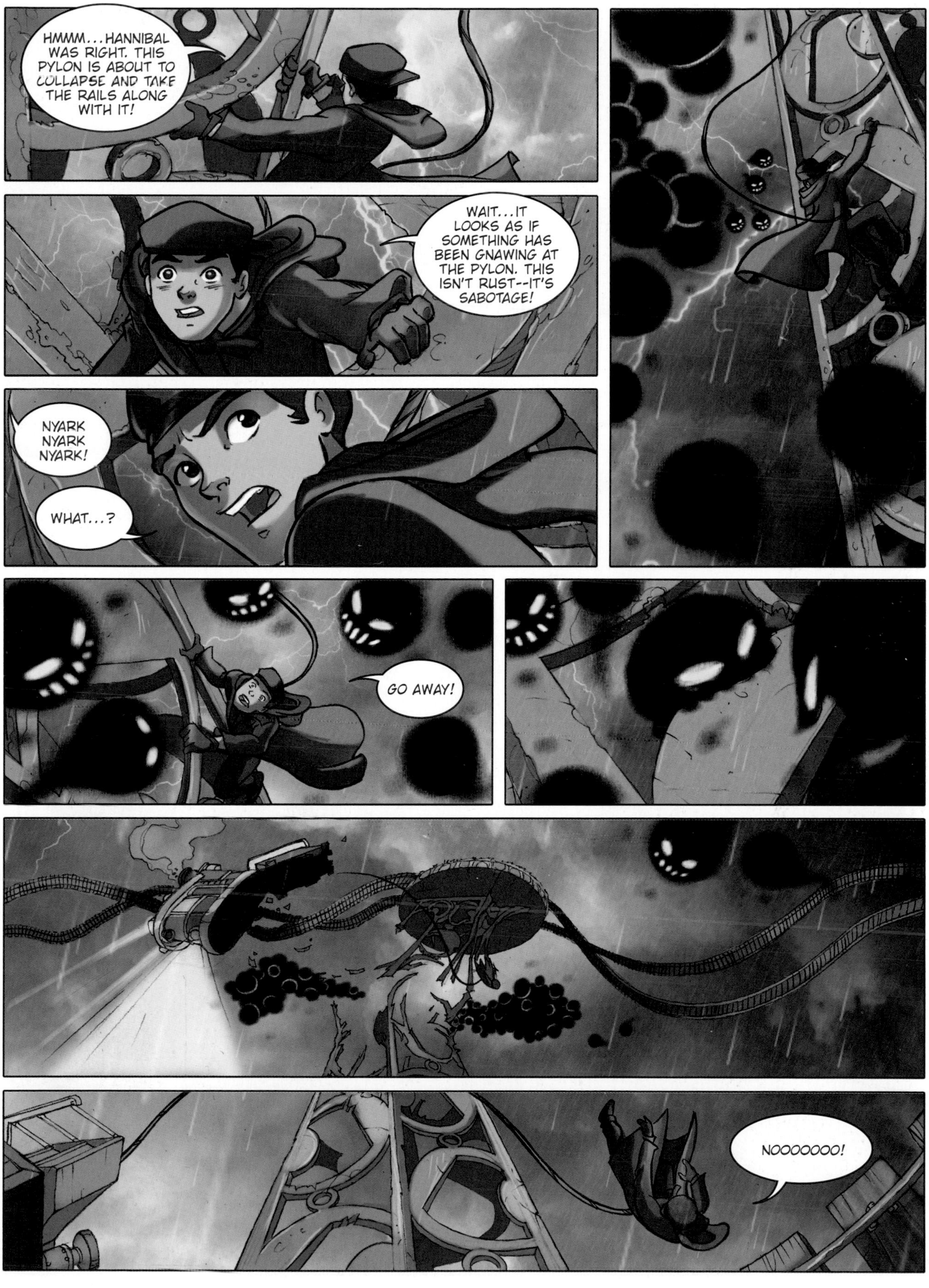
HMMM...HANNIBAL WAS RIGHT. THIS PYLON IS ABOUT TO COLLAPSE AND TAKE THE RAILS ALONG WITH IT!
WAIT...IT LOOKS AS IF SOMETHING HAS BEEN GNAWING AT THE PYLON. THIS ISN'T RUST--IT'S SABOTAGE!
NYARK NYARK NYARK!
WHAT...?
GO AWAY!
NOOOOOOO!

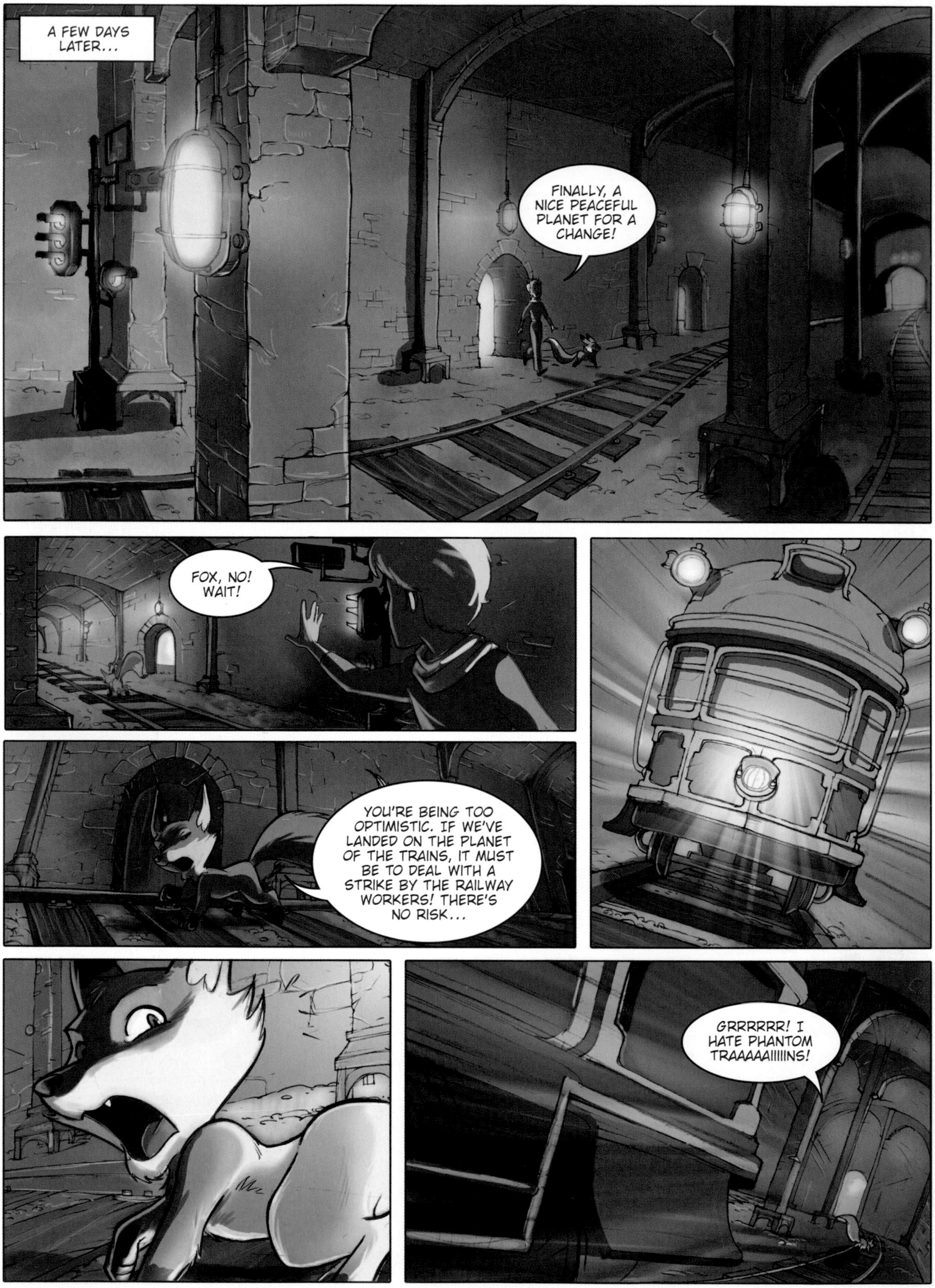
A FEW DAYS LATER...
FINALLY, A NICE PEACEFUL PLANET FOR A CHANGE!
FOX, NO! WAIT!
YOU'RE BEING TOO OPTIMISTIC. IF WE'VE LANDED ON THE PLANET OF THE TRAINS, IT MUST BE TO DEAL WITH A STRIKE BY THE RAILWAY WORKERS! THERE'S NO RISK...
GRRRRRR! I HATE PHANTOM TRAAAAAIIIIINS!

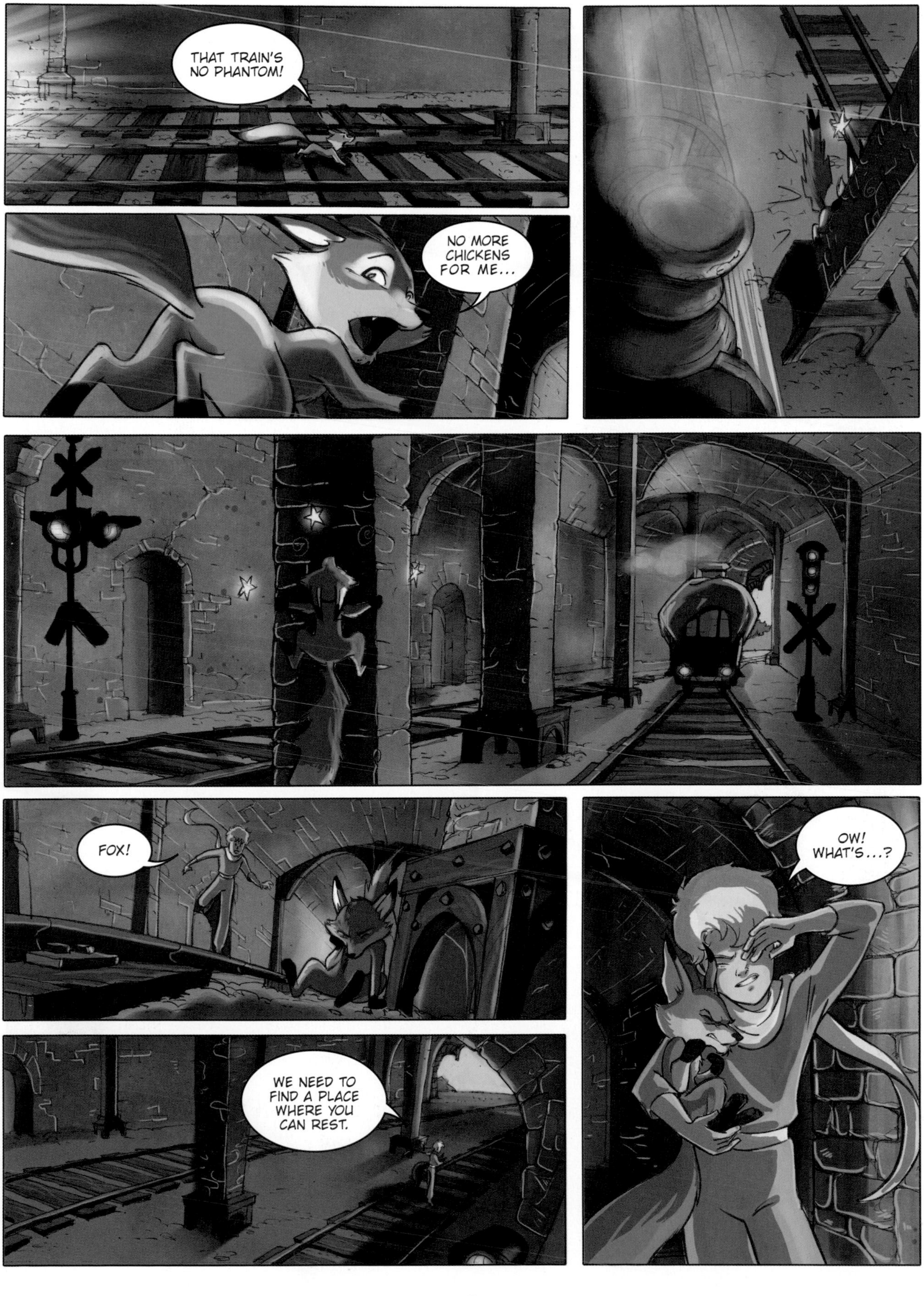
THAT TRAIN'S NO PHANTOM!
NO MORE CHICKENS FOR ME...
FOX!
WE NEED TO FIND A PLACE WHERE YOU CAN REST.
OW! WHAT'S...?

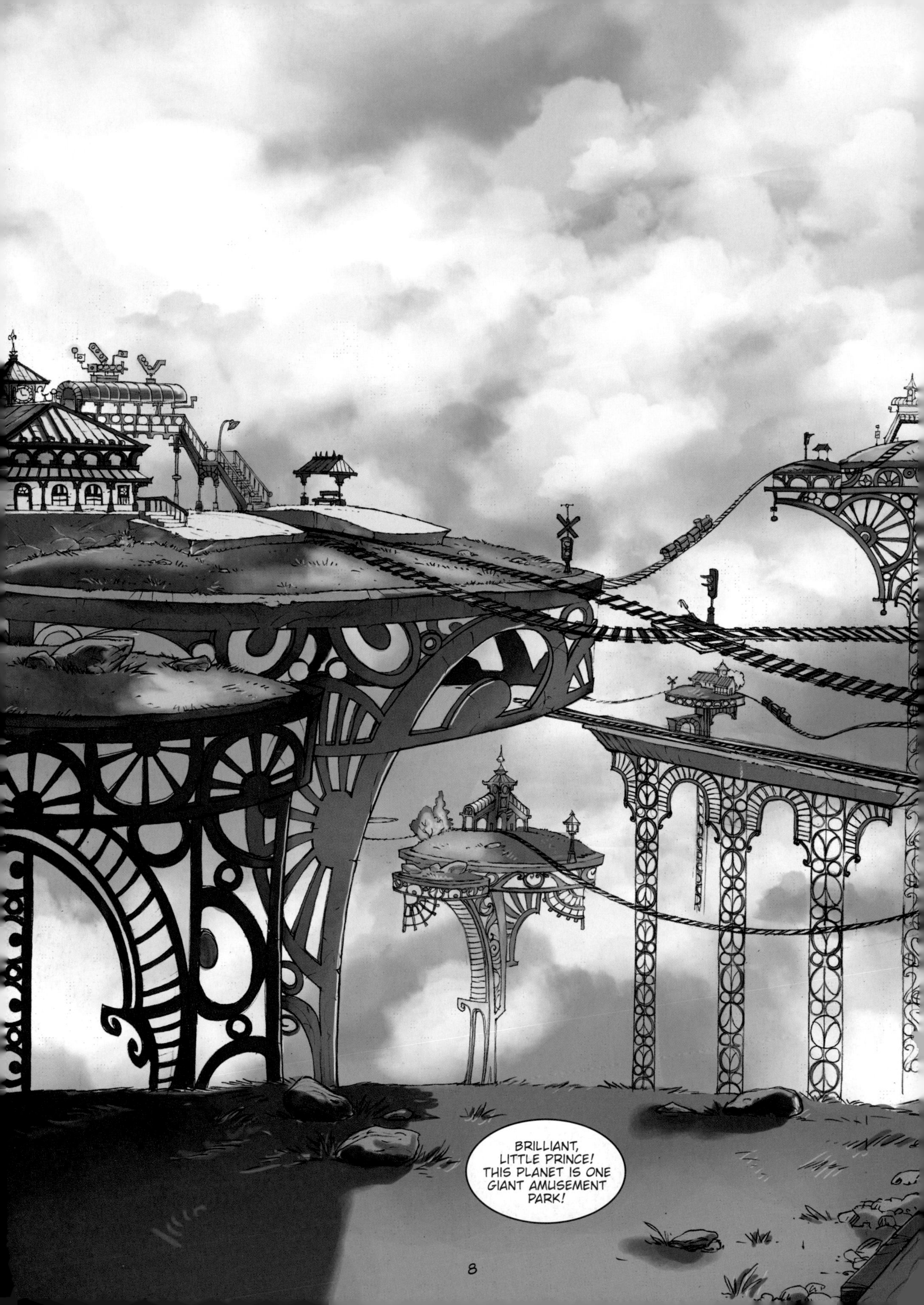
BRILLIANT, LITTLE PRINCE! THIS PLANET IS ONE GIANT AMUSEMENT PARK!

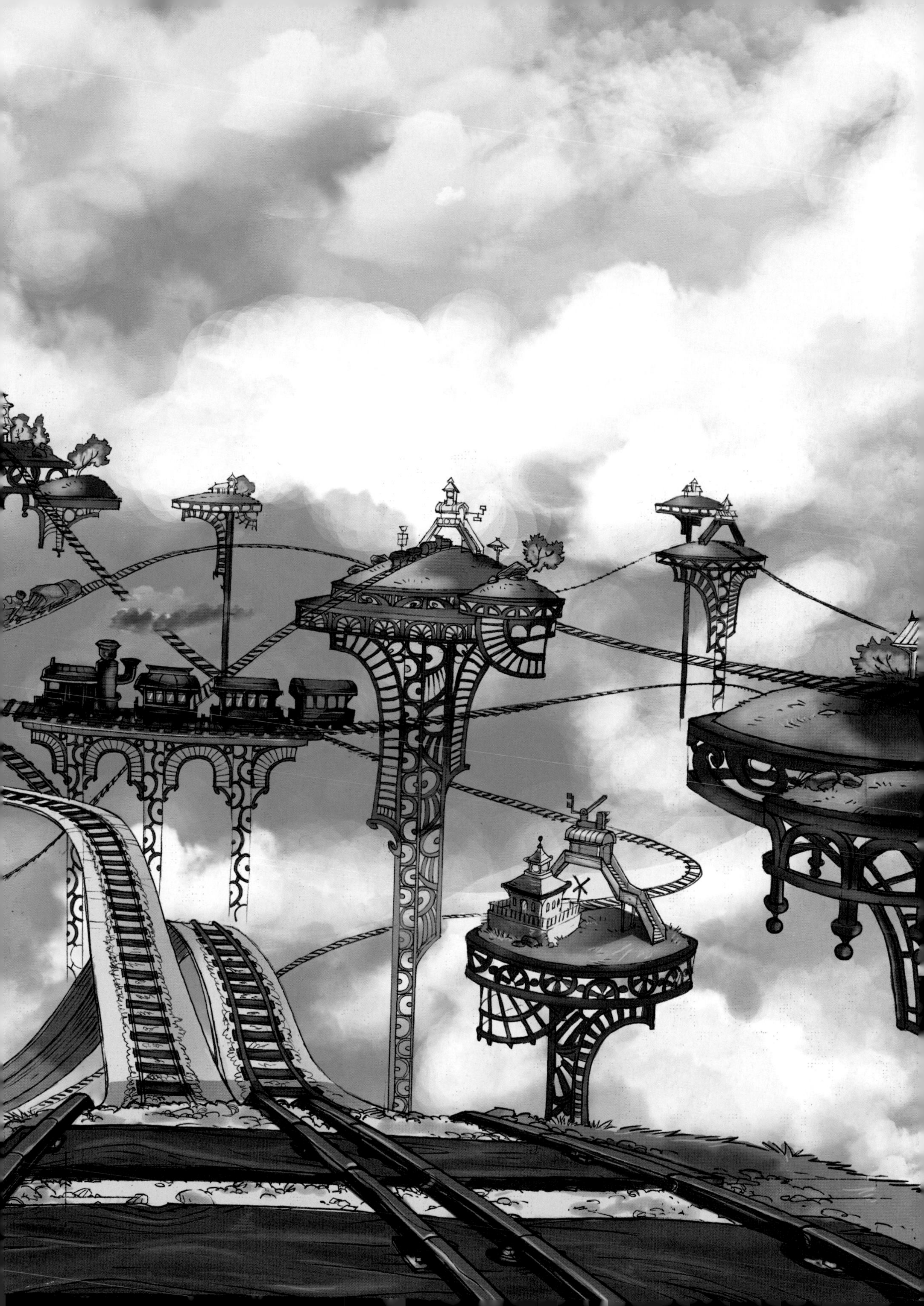

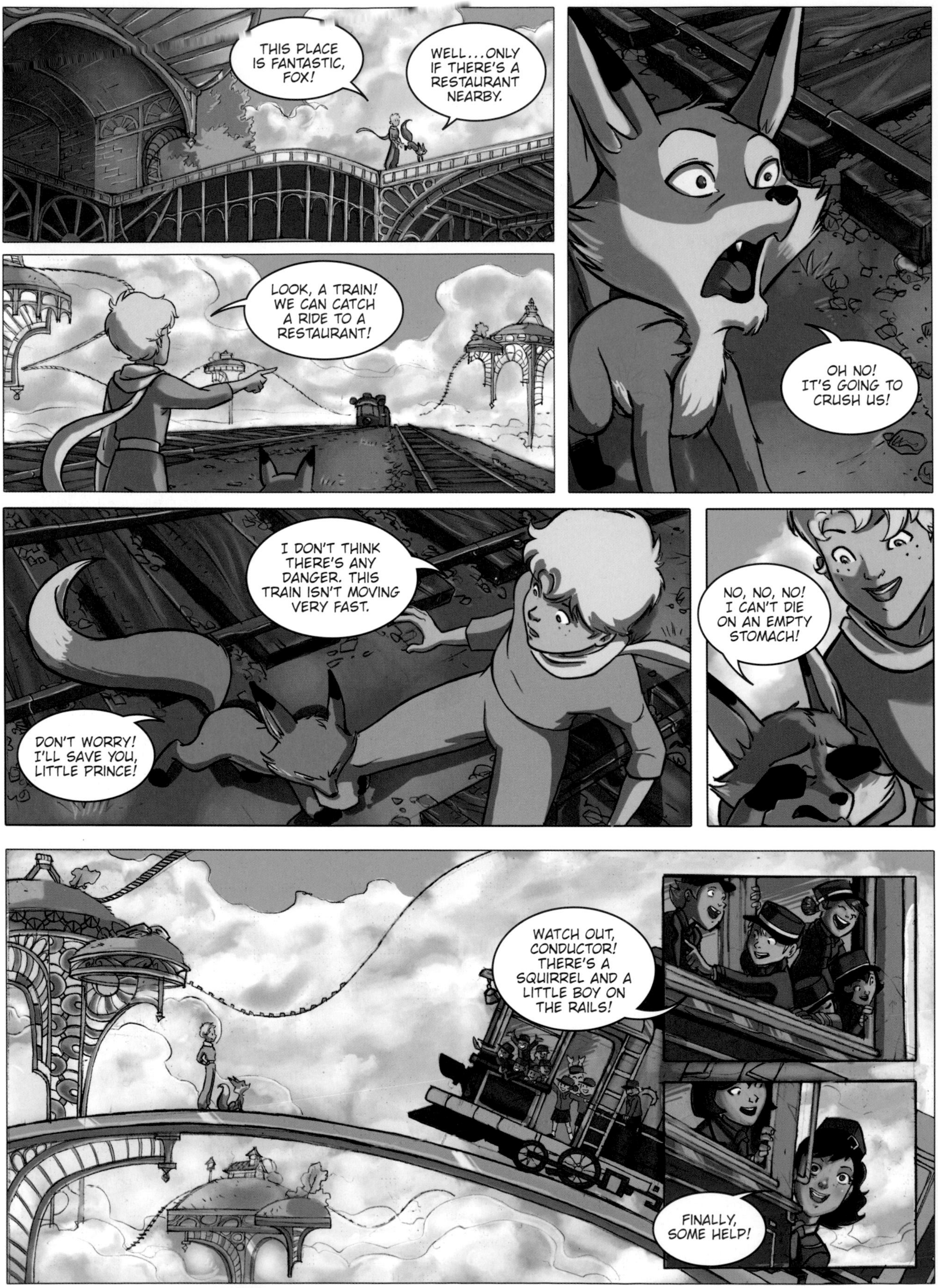
THIS PLACE IS FANTASTIC, FOX!
WELL...ONLY IF THERE'S A RESTAURANT NEARBY.
LOOK, A TRAIN! WE CAN CATCH A RIDE TO A RESTAURANT!
OH NO! IT'S GOING TO CRUSH US!
I DON'T THINK THERE'S ANY DANGER. THIS TRAIN ISN'T MOVING VERY FAST.
DON'T WORRY! I'LL SAVE YOU, LITTLE PRINCE!
NO, NO, NO! I CAN'T DIE ON AN EMPTY STOMACH!
WATCH OUT, CONDUCTOR! THERE'S A SQUIRREL AND A LITTLE BOY ON THE RAILS!
FINALLY, SOME HELP!

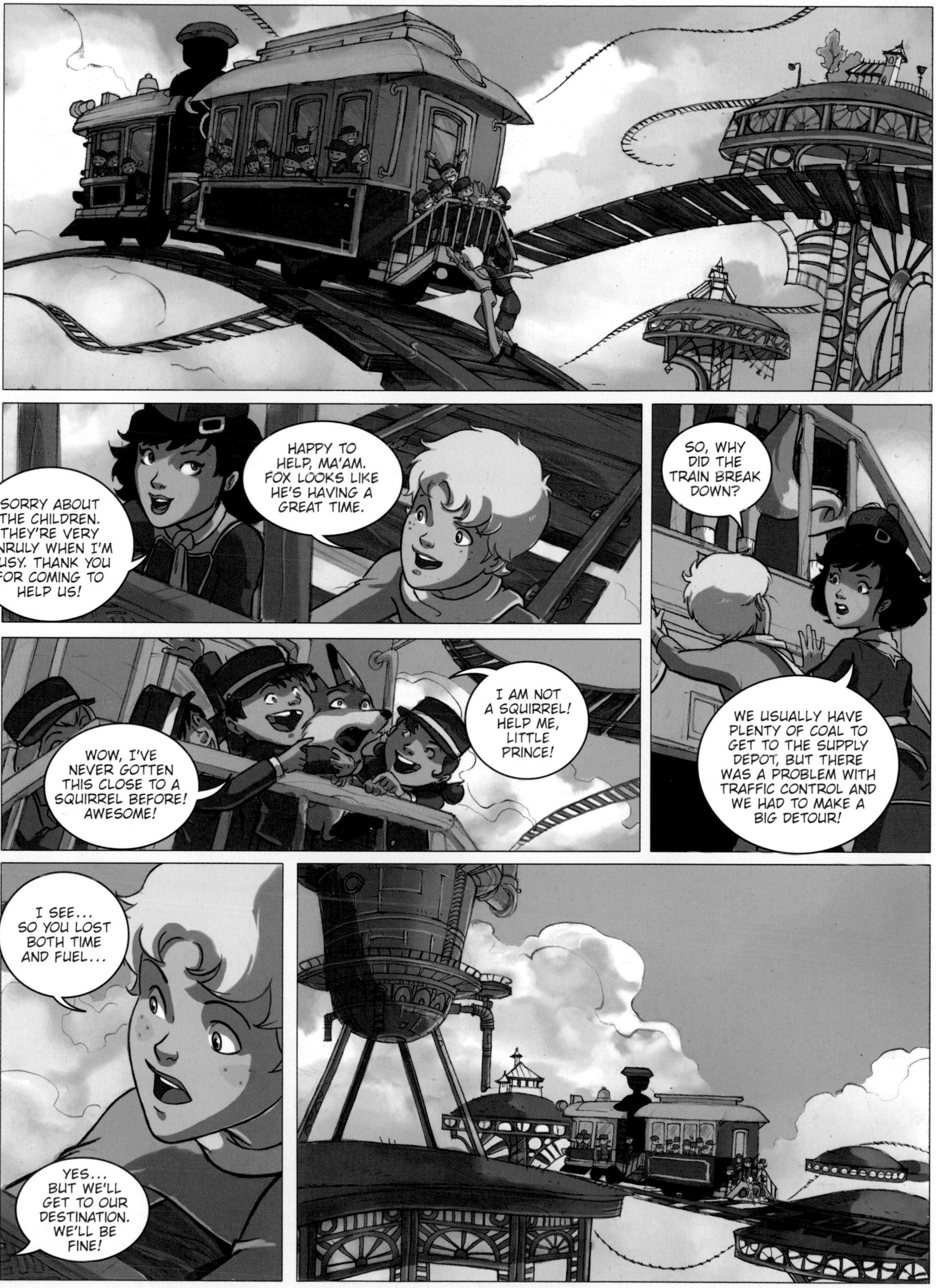
SORRY ABOUT THE CHILDREN. THEY'RE VERY UNRULY WHEN I'M BUSY. THANK YOU FOR COMING TO HELP US!
HAPPY TO HELP, MA'AM. FOX LOOKS LIKE HE'S HAVING A GREAT TIME.
WOW, I'VE NEVER GOTTEN THIS CLOSE TO A SQUIRREL BEFORE! AWESOME!
I AM NOT A SQUIRREL! HELP ME, LITTLE PRINCE!
SO, WHY DID THE TRAIN BREAK DOWN?
WE USUALLY HAVE PLENTY OF COAL TO GET TO THE SUPPLY DEPOT, BUT THERE WAS A PROBLEM WITH TRAFFIC CONTROL AND WE HAD TO MAKE A BIG DETOUR!
I SEE... SO YOU LOST BOTH TIME AND FUEL...
YES... BUT WE'LL GET TO OUR DESTINATION. WE'LL BE FINE!

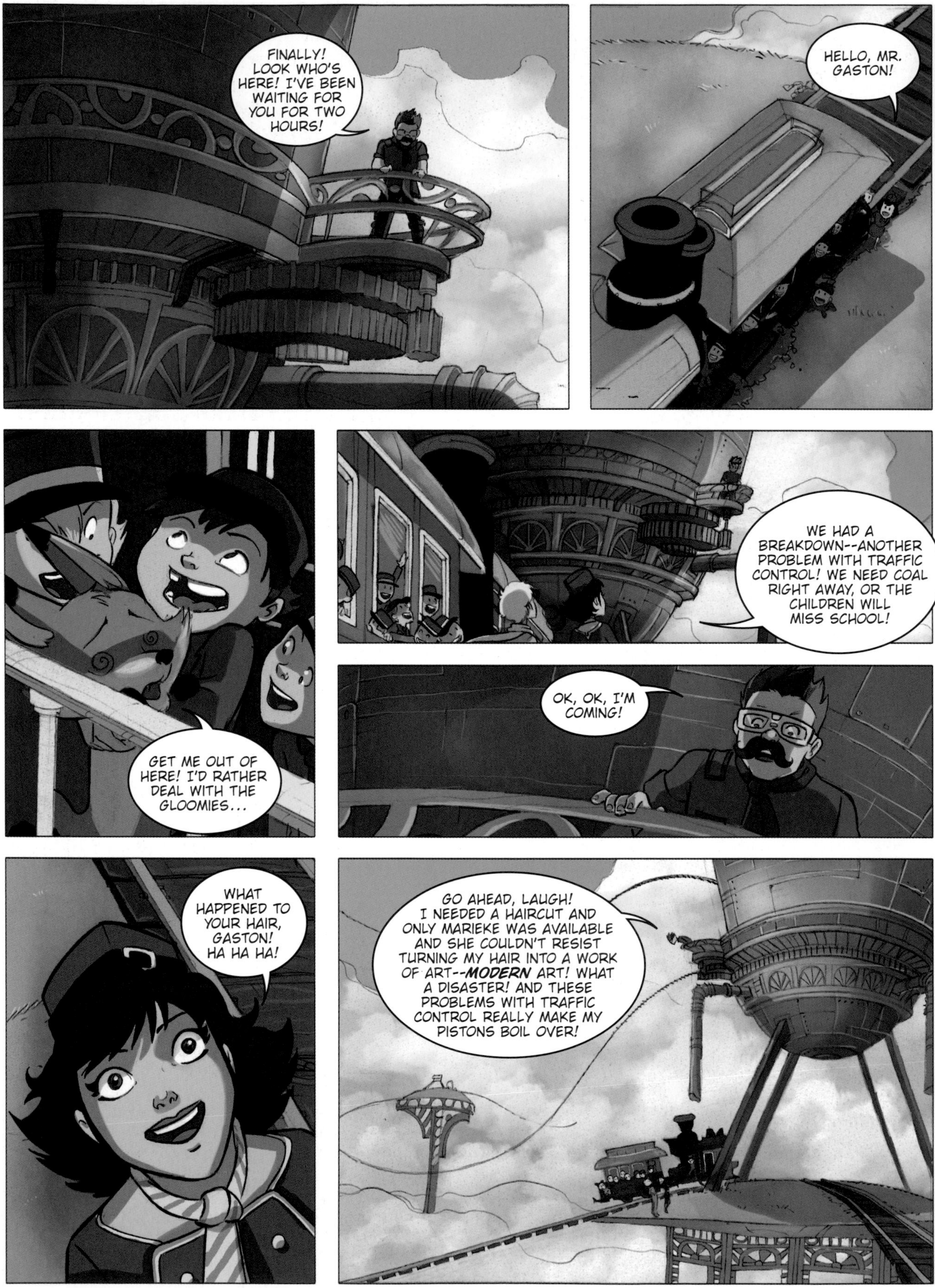

FINALLY! LOOK WHO'S HERE! I'VE BEEN WAITING FOR YOU FOR TWO HOURS!
HELLO, MR. GASTON!
GET ME OUT OF HERE! I'D RATHER DEAL WITH THE GLOOMIES...
WE HAD A BREAKDOWN--ANOTHER PROBLEM WITH TRAFFIC CONTROL! WE NEED COAL RIGHT AWAY, OR THE CHILDREN WILL MISS SCHOOL!
OK, OK, I'M COMING!
WHAT HAPPENED TO YOUR HAIR, GASTON! HA HA HA!
GO AHEAD, LAUGH! I NEEDED A HAIRCUT AND ONLY MARIEKE WAS AVAILABLE AND SHE COULDN'T RESIST TURNING MY HAIR INTO A WORK OF ART--*MODERN* ART! WHAT A DISASTER! AND THESE PROBLEMS WITH TRAFFIC CONTROL REALLY MAKE MY PISTONS BOIL OVER!

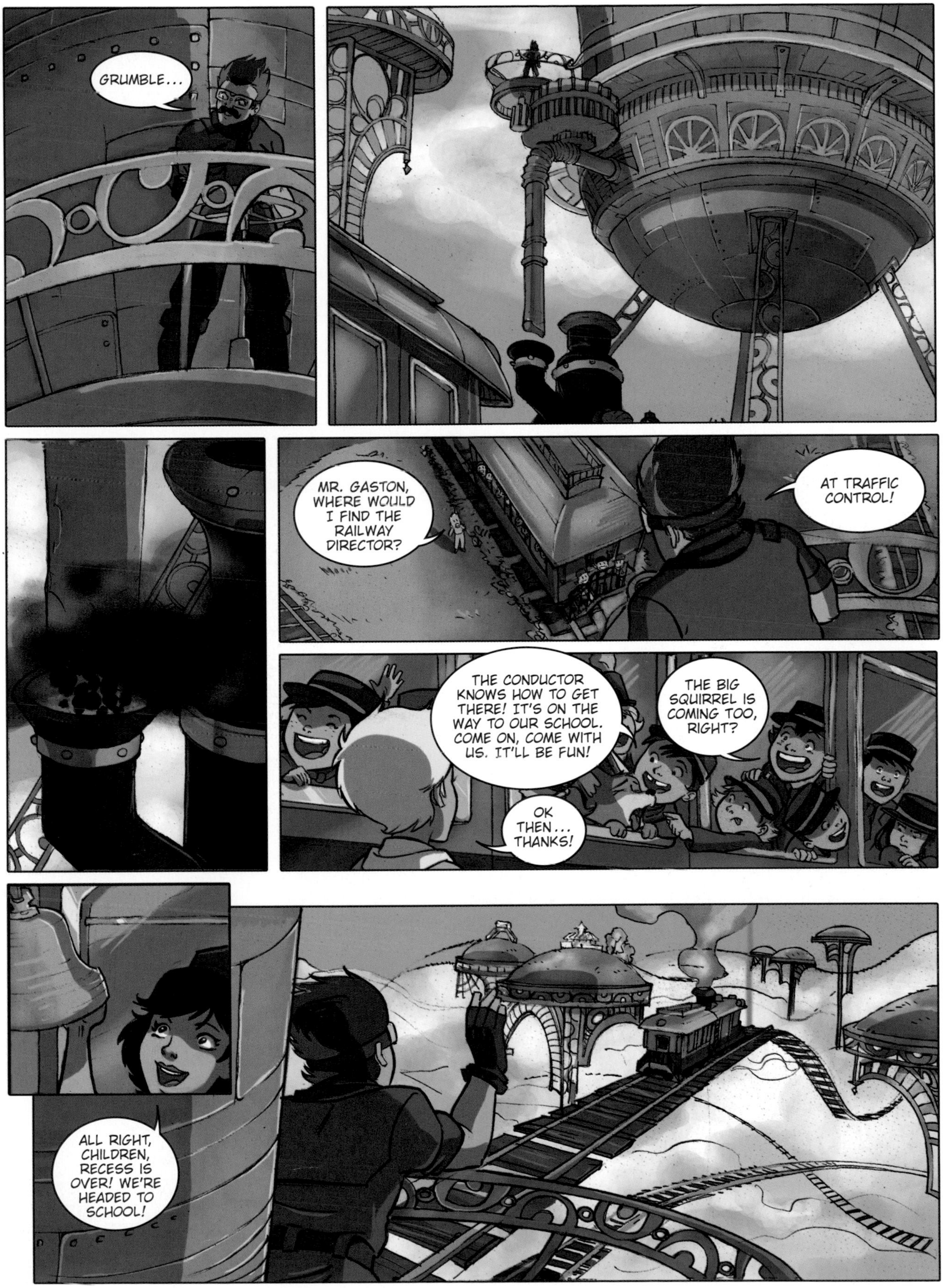
GRUMBLE...
MR. GASTON, WHERE WOULD I FIND THE RAILWAY DIRECTOR?
AT TRAFFIC CONTROL!
THE CONDUCTOR KNOWS HOW TO GET THERE! IT'S ON THE WAY TO OUR SCHOOL. COME ON, COME WITH US. IT'LL BE FUN!
THE BIG SQUIRREL IS COMING TOO, RIGHT?
OK THEN... THANKS!
ALL RIGHT, CHILDREN, RECESS IS OVER! WE'RE HEADED TO SCHOOL!

LOOK, IT'S TRAFFIC CONTROL!

THE RAILWAY STATION WILL HAVE FOOD, WON'T IT?

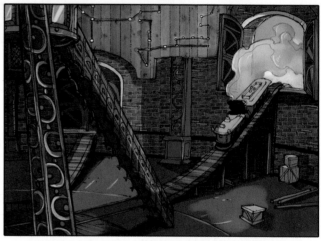

HANNIBAL, THE RAILWAY DIRECTOR, IS UP THERE IN TRAFFIC CONTROL. OLD HANNIBAL'S ALWAYS BEEN A BIT GROUCHY. ARE YOU SURE YOU WANT TO TALK WITH HIM?

THANKS FOR EVERYTHING, MA'AM! SEE YOU SOON.

WE'RE GOING TO MISS YOU, MR. BIG SQUIRREL! COME BACK SOON!

NOT IF I CAN HELP IT!

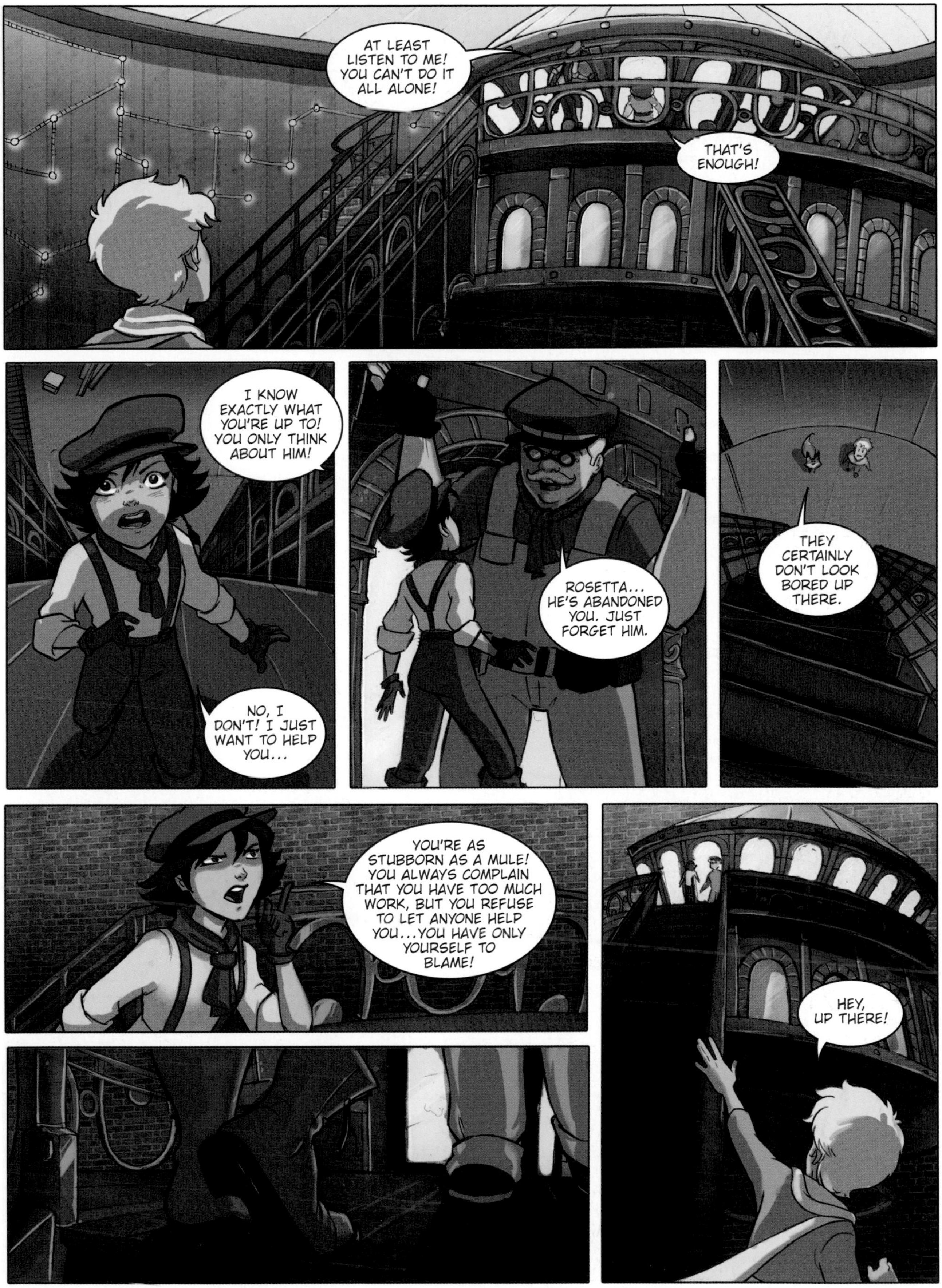
AT LEAST LISTEN TO ME! YOU CAN'T DO IT ALL ALONE!
THAT'S ENOUGH!
I KNOW EXACTLY WHAT YOU'RE UP TO! YOU ONLY THINK ABOUT HIM!
NO, I DON'T! I JUST WANT TO HELP YOU...
ROSETTA... HE'S ABANDONED YOU. JUST FORGET HIM.
THEY CERTAINLY DON'T LOOK BORED UP THERE.
YOU'RE AS STUBBORN AS A MULE! YOU ALWAYS COMPLAIN THAT YOU HAVE TOO MUCH WORK, BUT YOU REFUSE TO LET ANYONE HELP YOU...YOU HAVE ONLY YOURSELF TO BLAME!
HEY, UP THERE!

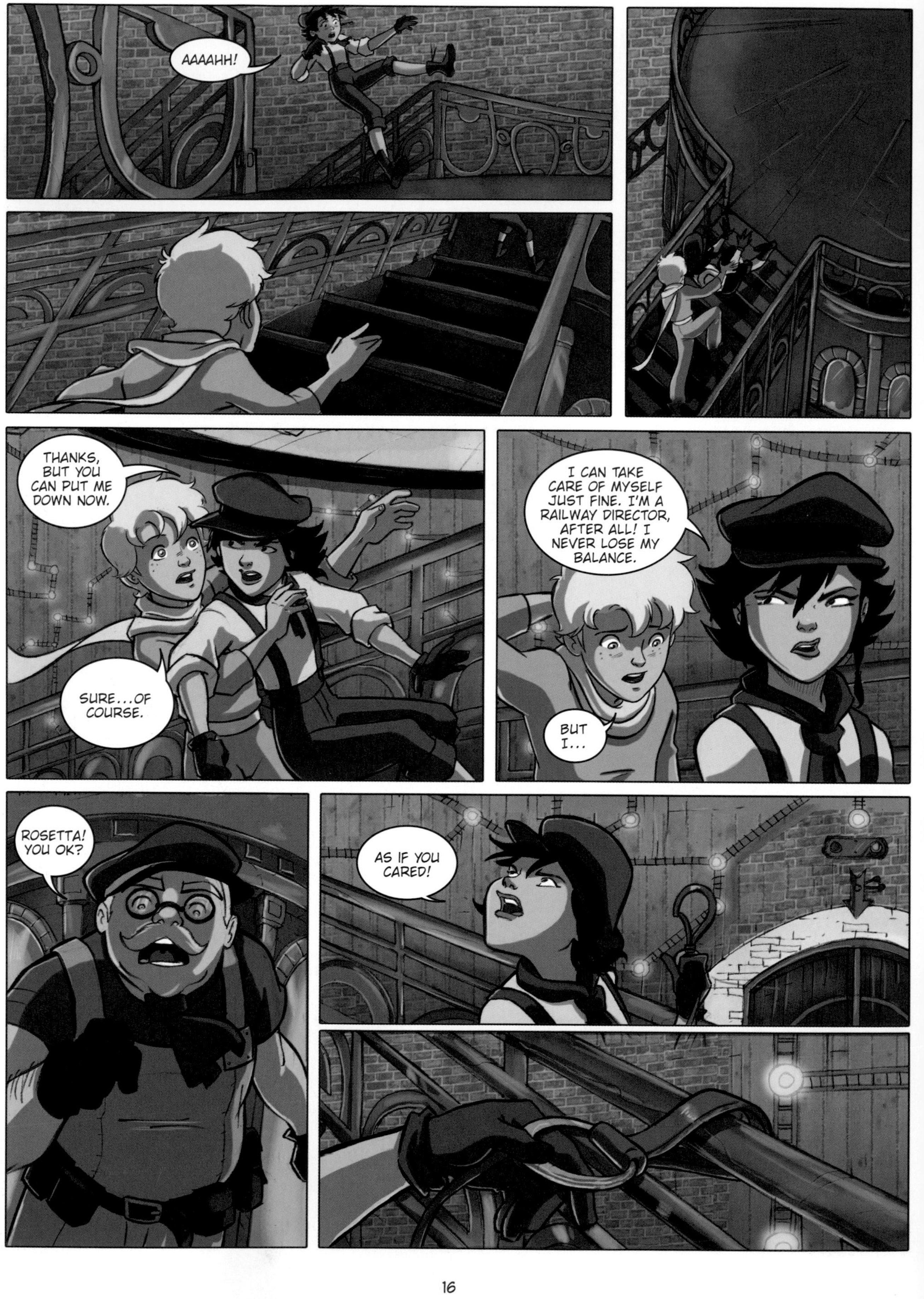
AAAAHH!
THANKS, BUT YOU CAN PUT ME DOWN NOW.
SURE...OF COURSE.
I CAN TAKE CARE OF MYSELF JUST FINE. I'M A RAILWAY DIRECTOR, AFTER ALL! I NEVER LOSE MY BALANCE.
BUT I...
ROSETTA! YOU OK?
AS IF YOU CARED!

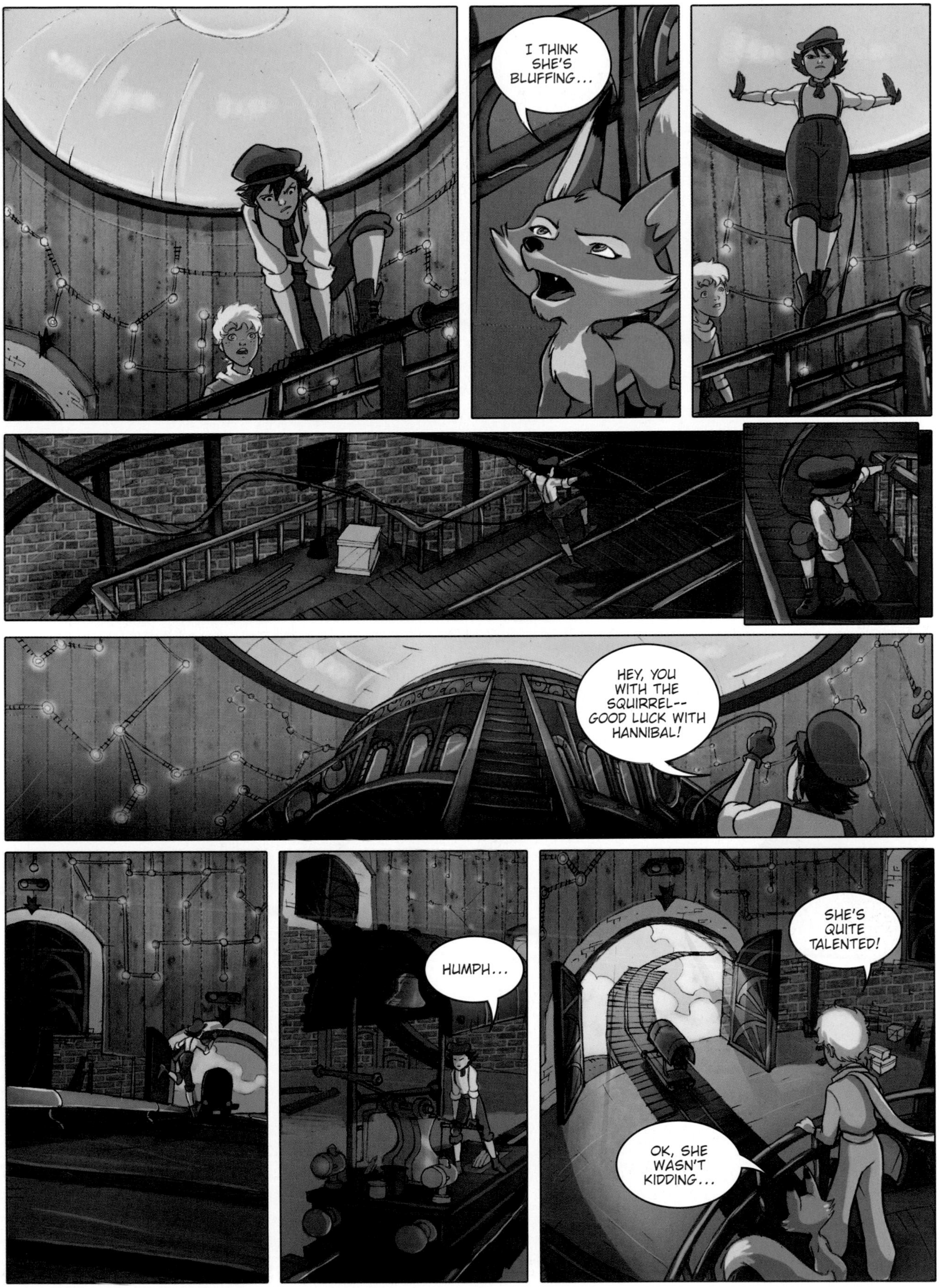
I THINK SHE'S BLUFFING...
HEY, YOU WITH THE SQUIRREL-- GOOD LUCK WITH HANNIBAL!
HUMPH...
SHE'S QUITE TALENTED!
OK, SHE WASN'T KIDDING...

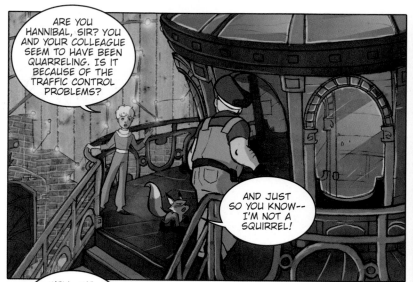

ARE YOU HANNIBAL, SIR? YOU AND YOUR COLLEAGUE SEEM TO HAVE BEEN QUARRELING. IS IT BECAUSE OF THE TRAFFIC CONTROL PROBLEMS?

AND JUST SO YOU KNOW-- I'M NOT A SQUIRREL!

BEAT IT, KID. I'VE GOT WORK TO DO!

WELL, WE DID WHAT WE COULD. IT'S NOT OUR FAULT HE WOULDN'T TALK TO US. CAN WE GO NOW?

NO, WAIT...

LEAVE ME ALONE!

WHAT HAVE I DONE? ROSETTA ALMOST GOT HURT, AND I SLAMMED THE DOOR IN THE FACE OF THAT NICE BOY AND HIS FUNNY-LOOKING SQUIRREL...MAYBE I SHOULD HAVE LISTENED TO THEM...

HSSS...YOU CAN'T DEPEND ON ANYONE ELSE TO KEEP THE RAILWAY SAFE...ALL THE OTHERS HAVE LET YOU DOWN. FOCUS ON YOUR WORK--NOTHING ELSE! IT'S YOUR DUTY.

HSSS...DON'T BE ANGRY WITH YOURSELF...HSSS...YOU HAVE NO CHOICE...ROSETTA IS IMPULSIVE...YOU CAN'T INDULGE HER EVERY WHIM WHEN THERE'S A WHOLE PLANET DEPENDING ON YOU!

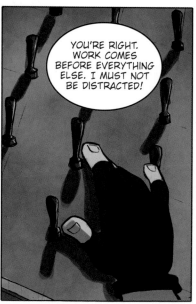

YOU'RE RIGHT. WORK COMES BEFORE EVERYTHING ELSE. I MUST NOT BE DISTRACTED!

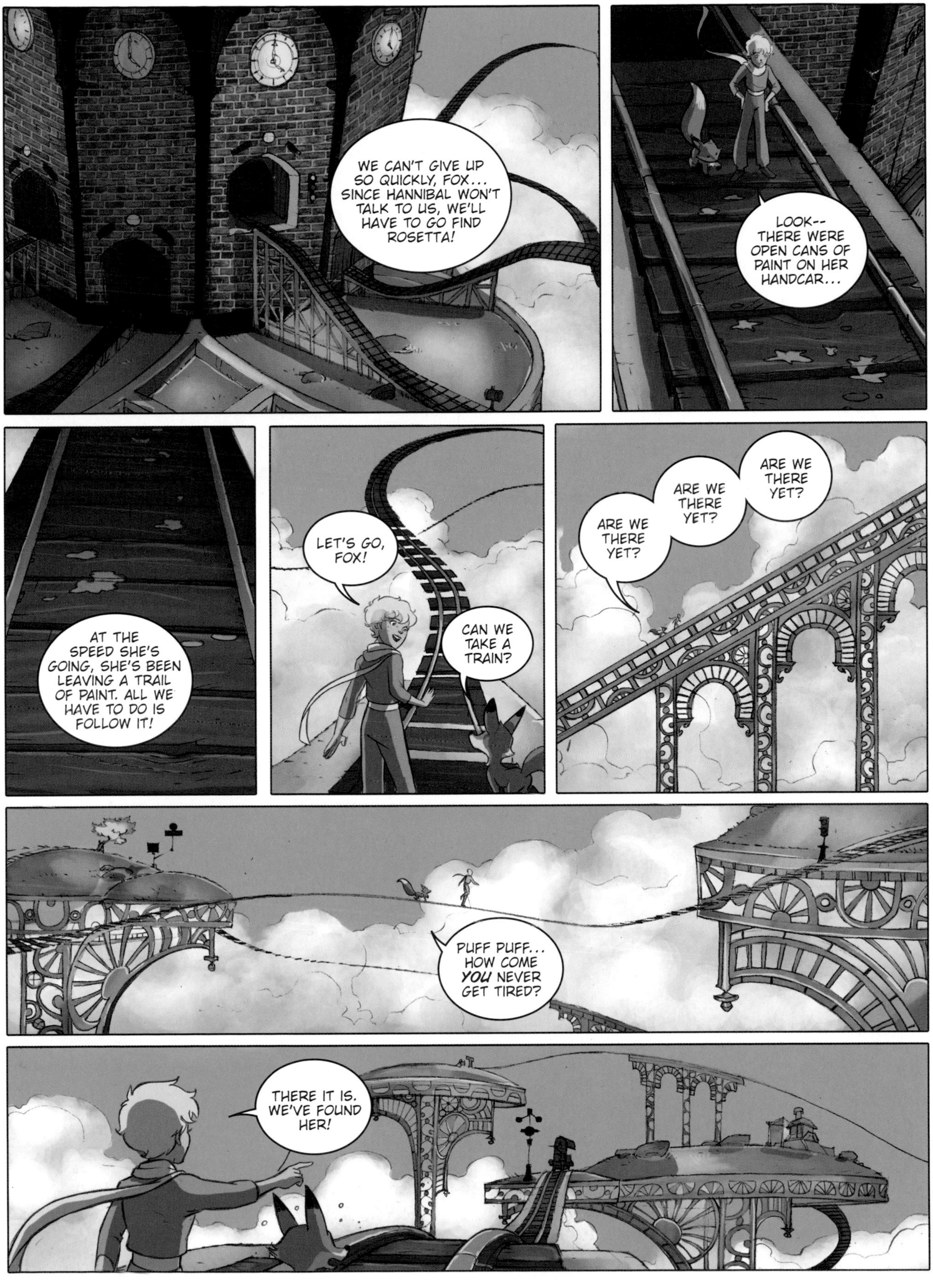
WE CAN'T GIVE UP SO QUICKLY, FOX... SINCE HANNIBAL WON'T TALK TO US, WE'LL HAVE TO GO FIND ROSETTA!
LOOK-- THERE WERE OPEN CANS OF PAINT ON HER HANDCAR...
AT THE SPEED SHE'S GOING, SHE'S BEEN LEAVING A TRAIL OF PAINT. ALL WE HAVE TO DO IS FOLLOW IT!
LET'S GO, FOX!
CAN WE TAKE A TRAIN?
ARE WE THERE YET?
ARE WE THERE YET?
ARE WE THERE YET?
PUFF PUFF... HOW COME YOU NEVER GET TIRED?
THERE IT IS. WE'VE FOUND HER!

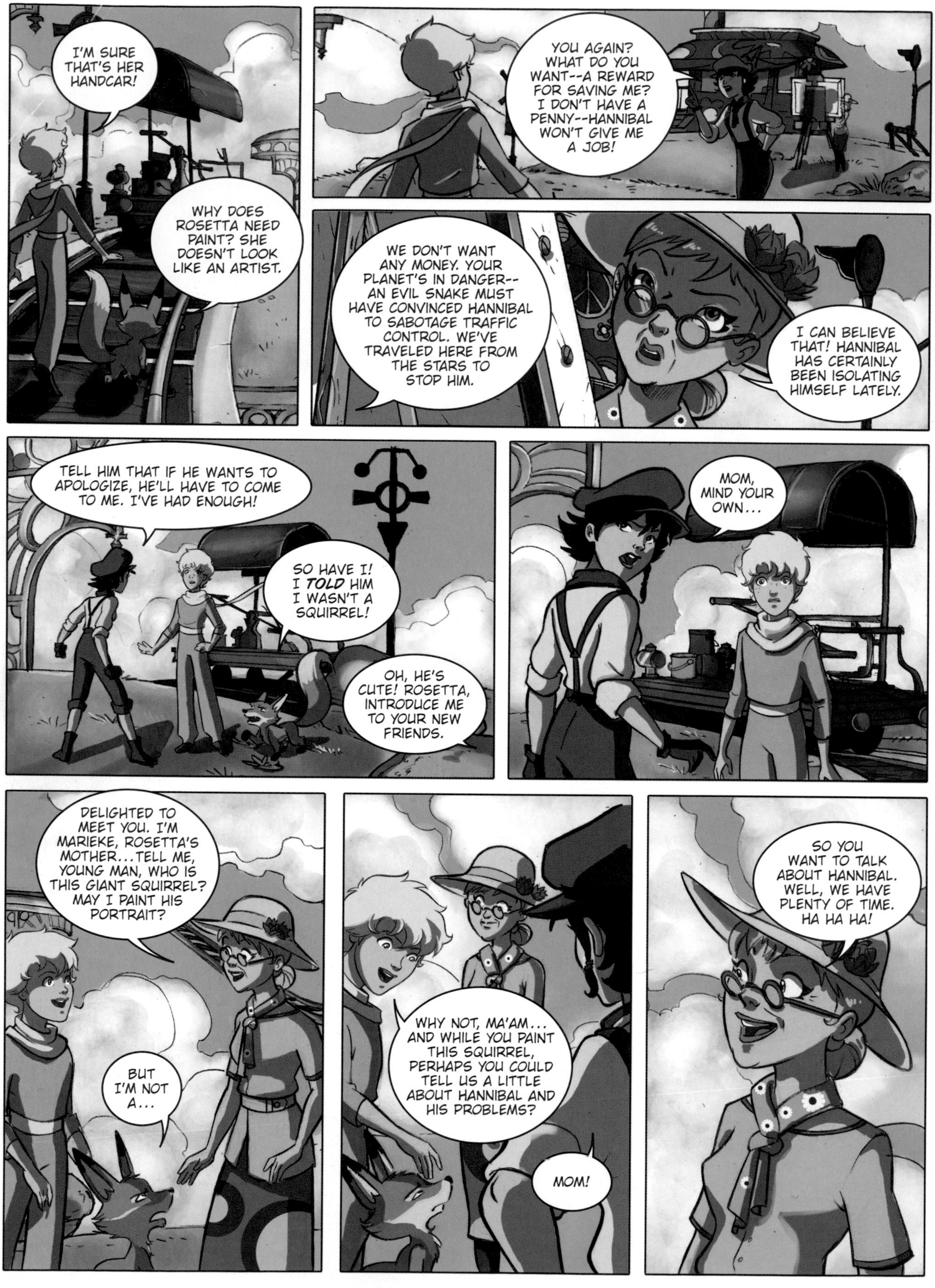
I'M SURE THAT'S HER HANDCAR!
WHY DOES ROSETTA NEED PAINT? SHE DOESN'T LOOK LIKE AN ARTIST.
YOU AGAIN? WHAT DO YOU WANT--A REWARD FOR SAVING ME? I DON'T HAVE A PENNY--HANNIBAL WON'T GIVE ME A JOB!
WE DON'T WANT ANY MONEY. YOUR PLANET'S IN DANGER--AN EVIL SNAKE MUST HAVE CONVINCED HANNIBAL TO SABOTAGE TRAFFIC CONTROL. WE'VE TRAVELED HERE FROM THE STARS TO STOP HIM.
I CAN BELIEVE THAT! HANNIBAL HAS CERTAINLY BEEN ISOLATING HIMSELF LATELY.
TELL HIM THAT IF HE WANTS TO APOLOGIZE, HE'LL HAVE TO COME TO ME. I'VE HAD ENOUGH!
SO HAVE I! I *TOLD* HIM I WASN'T A SQUIRREL!
OH, HE'S CUTE! ROSETTA, INTRODUCE ME TO YOUR NEW FRIENDS.
MOM, MIND YOUR OWN...
DELIGHTED TO MEET YOU. I'M MARIEKE, ROSETTA'S MOTHER...TELL ME, YOUNG MAN, WHO IS THIS GIANT SQUIRREL? MAY I PAINT HIS PORTRAIT?
BUT I'M NOT A...
WHY NOT, MA'AM... AND WHILE YOU PAINT THIS SQUIRREL, PERHAPS YOU COULD TELL US A LITTLE ABOUT HANNIBAL AND HIS PROBLEMS?
MOM!
SO YOU WANT TO TALK ABOUT HANNIBAL. WELL, WE HAVE PLENTY OF TIME. HA HA HA!

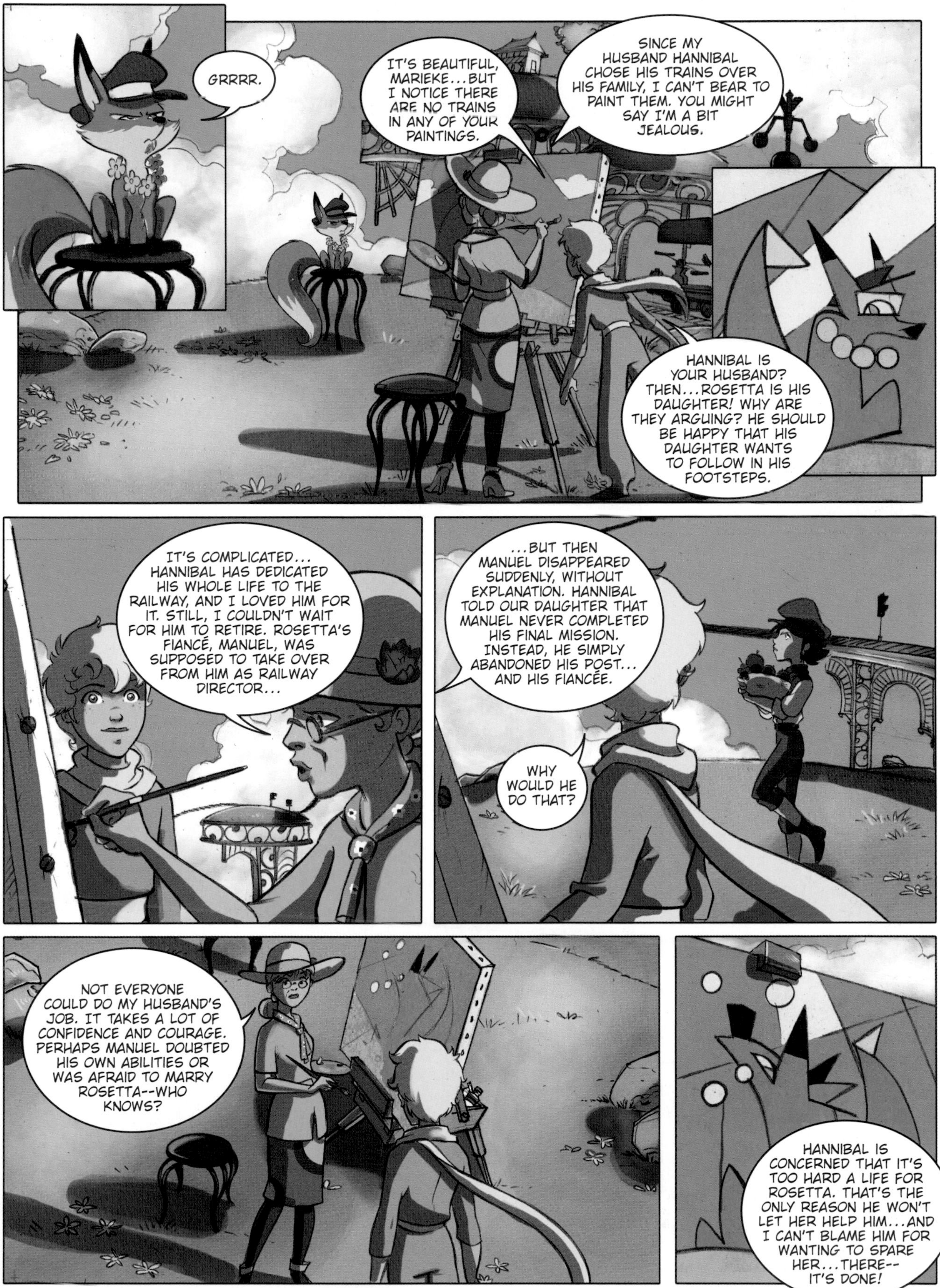
GRRRR.
IT'S BEAUTIFUL, MARIEKE...BUT I NOTICE THERE ARE NO TRAINS IN ANY OF YOUR PAINTINGS.
SINCE MY HUSBAND HANNIBAL CHOSE HIS TRAINS OVER HIS FAMILY, I CAN'T BEAR TO PAINT THEM. YOU MIGHT SAY I'M A BIT JEALOUS.
HANNIBAL IS YOUR HUSBAND? THEN...ROSETTA IS HIS DAUGHTER! WHY ARE THEY ARGUING? HE SHOULD BE HAPPY THAT HIS DAUGHTER WANTS TO FOLLOW IN HIS FOOTSTEPS.
IT'S COMPLICATED... HANNIBAL HAS DEDICATED HIS WHOLE LIFE TO THE RAILWAY, AND I LOVED HIM FOR IT. STILL, I COULDN'T WAIT FOR HIM TO RETIRE. ROSETTA'S FIANCÉ, MANUEL, WAS SUPPOSED TO TAKE OVER FROM HIM AS RAILWAY DIRECTOR...
...BUT THEN MANUEL DISAPPEARED SUDDENLY, WITHOUT EXPLANATION. HANNIBAL TOLD OUR DAUGHTER THAT MANUEL NEVER COMPLETED HIS FINAL MISSION. INSTEAD, HE SIMPLY ABANDONED HIS POST... AND HIS FIANCÉE.
WHY WOULD HE DO THAT?
NOT EVERYONE COULD DO MY HUSBAND'S JOB. IT TAKES A LOT OF CONFIDENCE AND COURAGE. PERHAPS MANUEL DOUBTED HIS OWN ABILITIES OR WAS AFRAID TO MARRY ROSETTA--WHO KNOWS?
HANNIBAL IS CONCERNED THAT IT'S TOO HARD A LIFE FOR ROSETTA. THAT'S THE ONLY REASON HE WON'T LET HER HELP HIM...AND I CAN'T BLAME HIM FOR WANTING TO SPARE HER...THERE-- IT'S DONE!

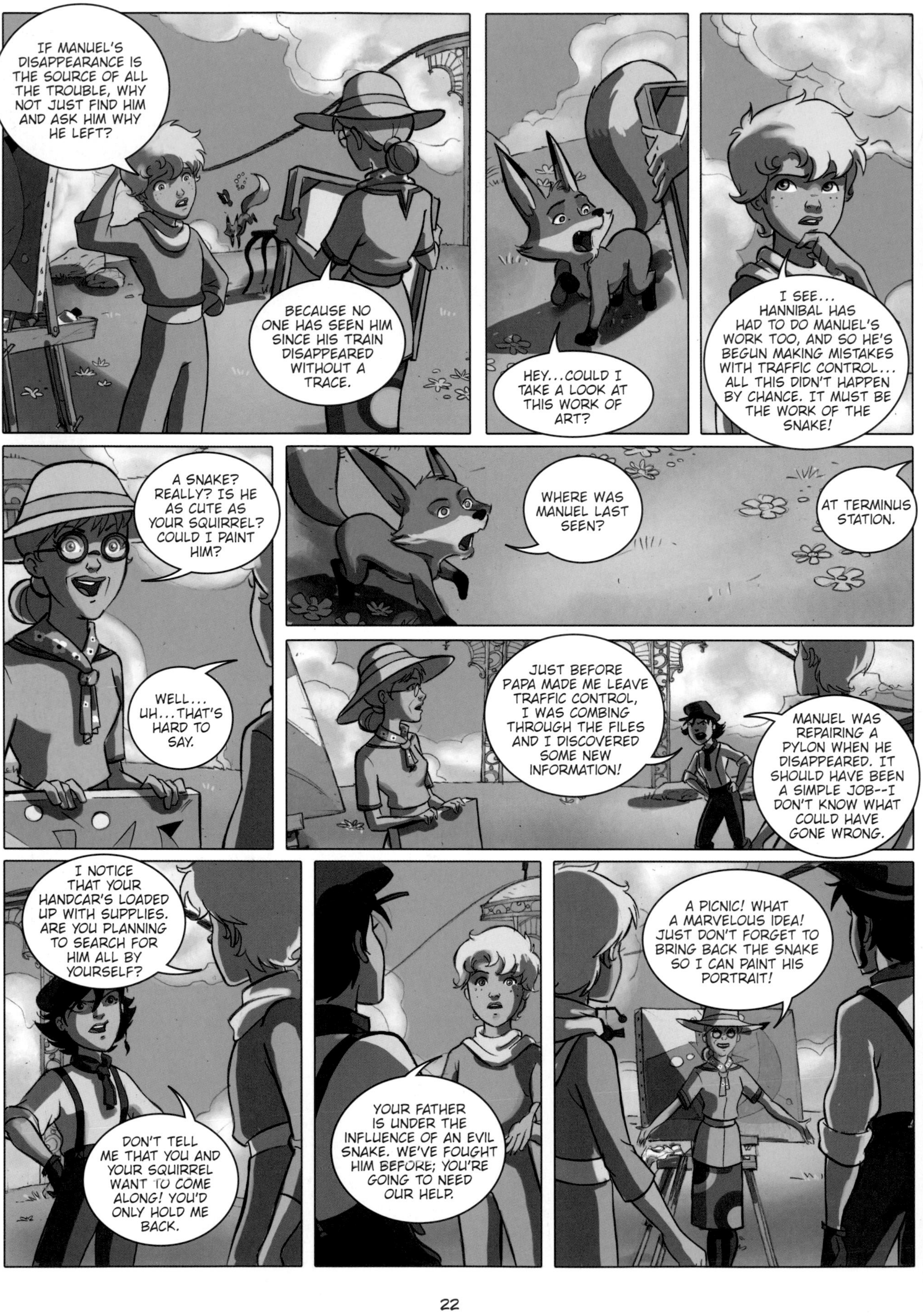
IF MANUEL'S DISAPPEARANCE IS THE SOURCE OF ALL THE TROUBLE, WHY NOT JUST FIND HIM AND ASK HIM WHY HE LEFT?
BECAUSE NO ONE HAS SEEN HIM SINCE HIS TRAIN DISAPPEARED WITHOUT A TRACE.
HEY...COULD I TAKE A LOOK AT THIS WORK OF ART?
I SEE... HANNIBAL HAS HAD TO DO MANUEL'S WORK TOO, AND SO HE'S BEGUN MAKING MISTAKES WITH TRAFFIC CONTROL... ALL THIS DIDN'T HAPPEN BY CHANCE. IT MUST BE THE WORK OF THE SNAKE!
A SNAKE? REALLY? IS HE AS CUTE AS YOUR SQUIRREL? COULD I PAINT HIM?
WELL... UH...THAT'S HARD TO SAY.
WHERE WAS MANUEL LAST SEEN?
AT TERMINUS STATION.
JUST BEFORE PAPA MADE ME LEAVE TRAFFIC CONTROL, I WAS COMBING THROUGH THE FILES AND I DISCOVERED SOME NEW INFORMATION!
MANUEL WAS REPAIRING A PYLON WHEN HE DISAPPEARED. IT SHOULD HAVE BEEN A SIMPLE JOB--I DON'T KNOW WHAT COULD HAVE GONE WRONG.
I NOTICE THAT YOUR HANDCAR'S LOADED UP WITH SUPPLIES. ARE YOU PLANNING TO SEARCH FOR HIM ALL BY YOURSELF?
DON'T TELL ME THAT YOU AND YOUR SQUIRREL WANT TO COME ALONG! YOU'D ONLY HOLD ME BACK.
YOUR FATHER IS UNDER THE INFLUENCE OF AN EVIL SNAKE. WE'VE FOUGHT HIM BEFORE; YOU'RE GOING TO NEED OUR HELP.
A PICNIC! WHAT A MARVELOUS IDEA! JUST DON'T FORGET TO BRING BACK THE SNAKE SO I CAN PAINT HIS PORTRAIT!

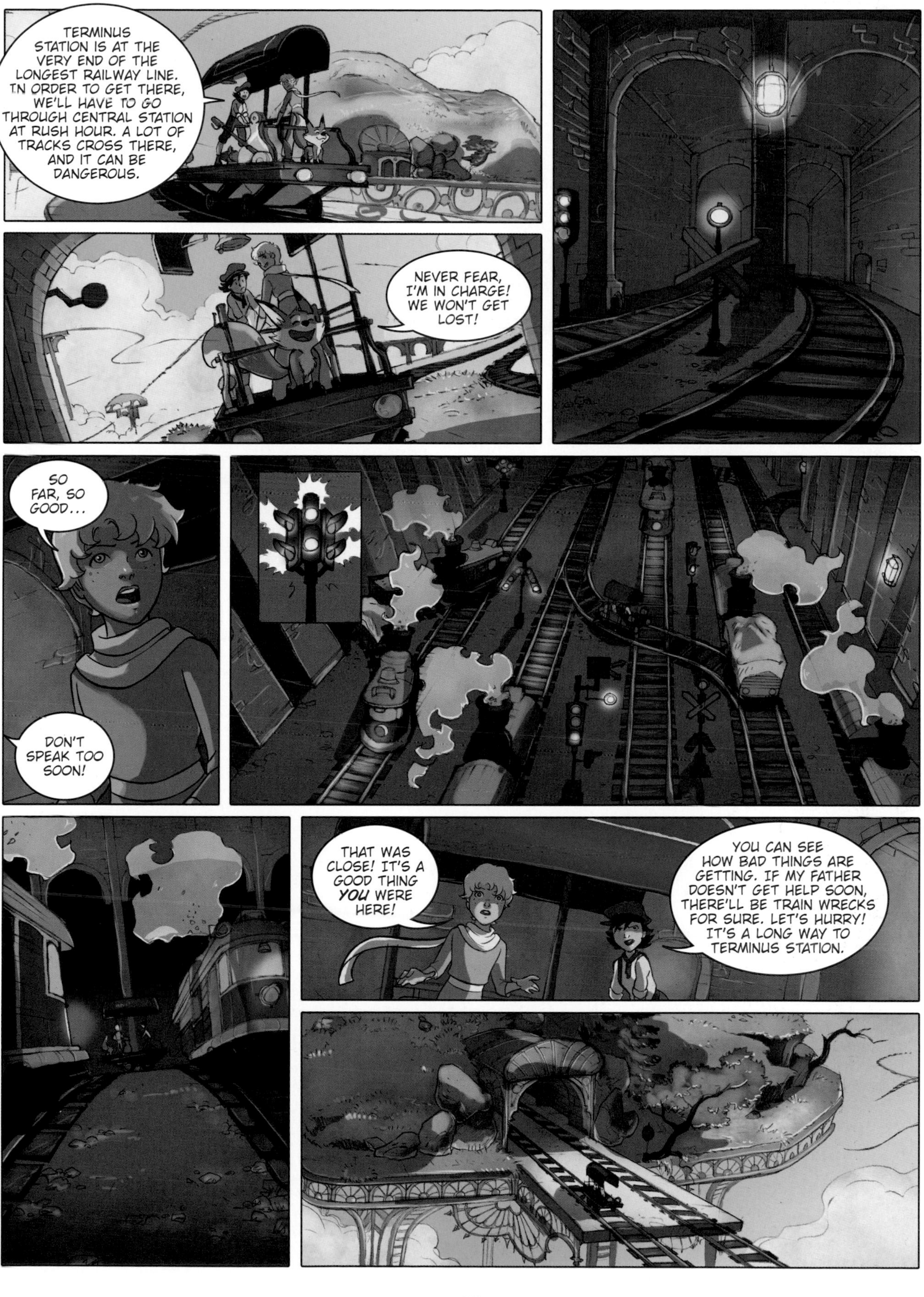
TERMINUS STATION IS AT THE VERY END OF THE LONGEST RAILWAY LINE. IN ORDER TO GET THERE, WE'LL HAVE TO GO THROUGH CENTRAL STATION AT RUSH HOUR. A LOT OF TRACKS CROSS THERE, AND IT CAN BE DANGEROUS.
NEVER FEAR, I'M IN CHARGE! WE WON'T GET LOST!
SO FAR, SO GOOD...
DON'T SPEAK TOO SOON!
THAT WAS CLOSE! IT'S A GOOD THING *YOU* WERE HERE!
YOU CAN SEE HOW BAD THINGS ARE GETTING. IF MY FATHER DOESN'T GET HELP SOON, THERE'LL BE TRAIN WRECKS FOR SURE. LET'S HURRY! IT'S A LONG WAY TO TERMINUS STATION.

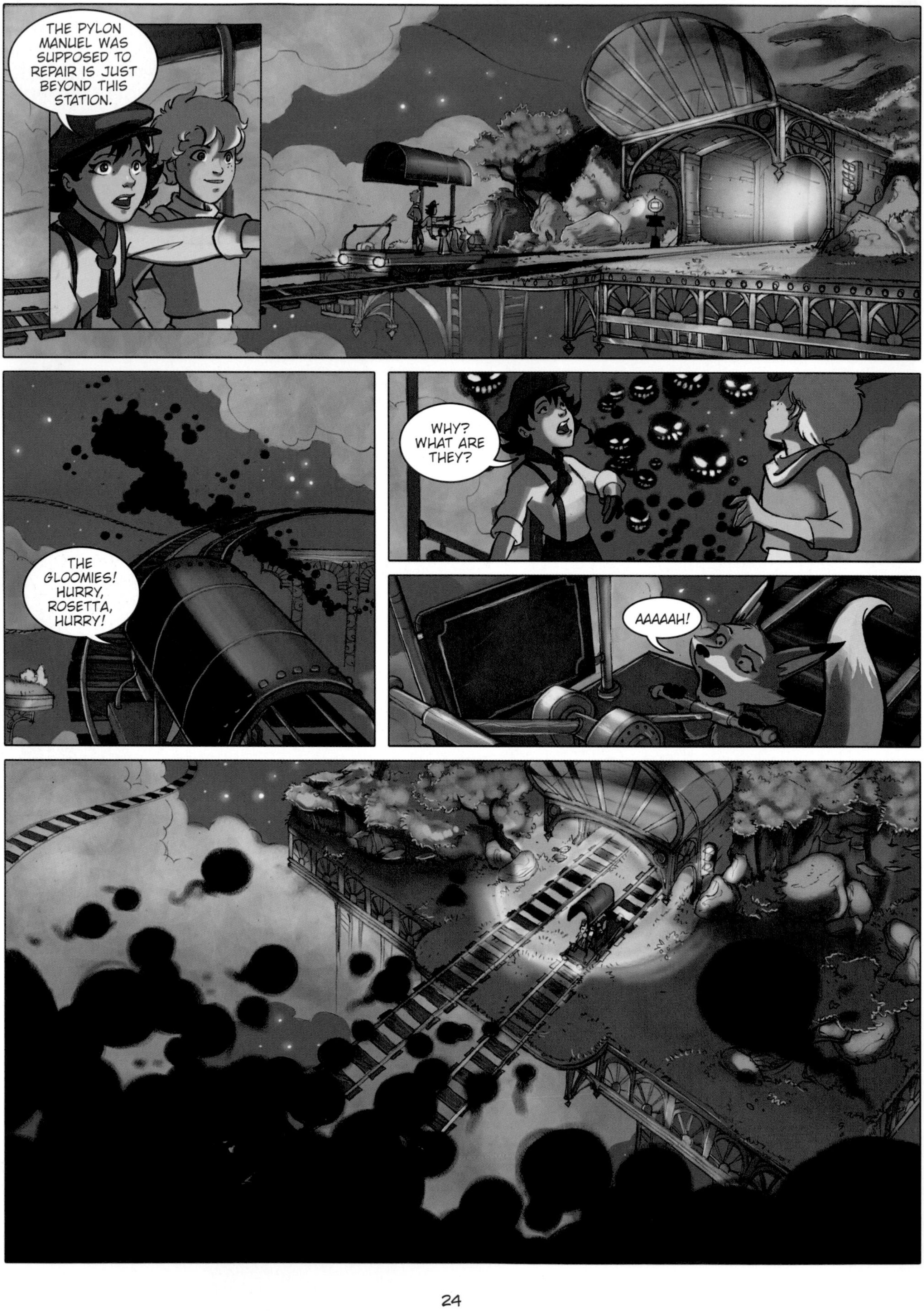
THE PYLON MANUEL WAS SUPPOSED TO REPAIR IS JUST BEYOND THIS STATION.
WHY? WHAT ARE THEY?
THE GLOOMIES! HURRY, ROSETTA, HURRY!
AAAAAH!

FASTER, FOX! THEY'RE GAINING ON US!

I'LL TRY!

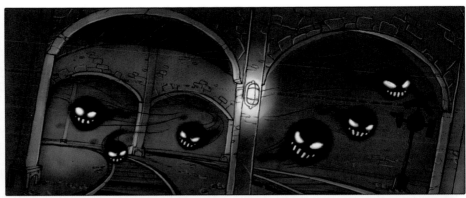

WE'RE TRAPPED!

FULL SPEED AHEAD! I'LL TAKE CARE OF THEM!

GOOD JOB!

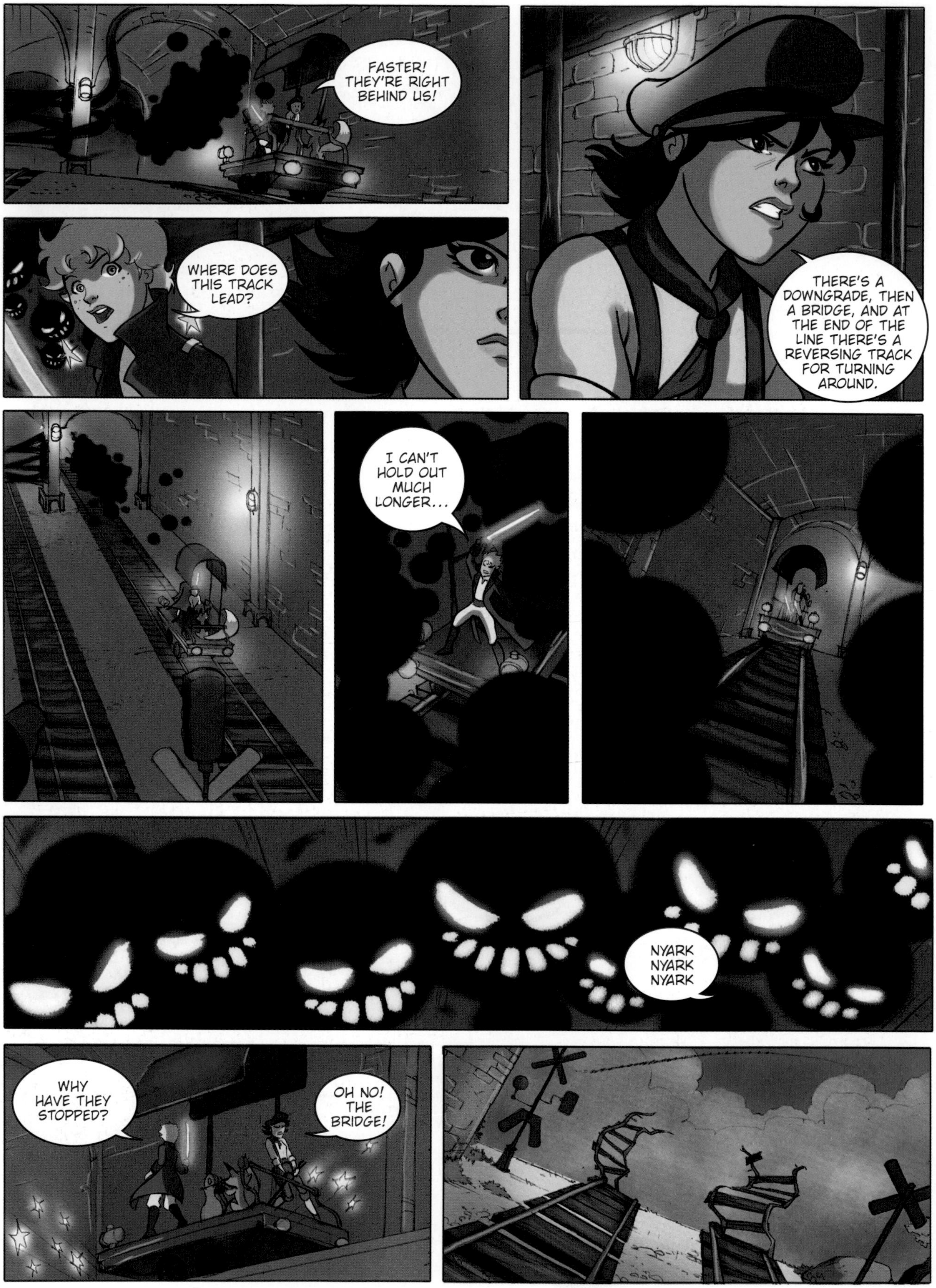
FASTER! THEY'RE RIGHT BEHIND US!
WHERE DOES THIS TRACK LEAD?
THERE'S A DOWNGRADE, THEN A BRIDGE, AND AT THE END OF THE LINE THERE'S A REVERSING TRACK FOR TURNING AROUND.
I CAN'T HOLD OUT MUCH LONGER...
NYARK NYARK NYARK
WHY HAVE THEY STOPPED?
OH NO! THE BRIDGE!

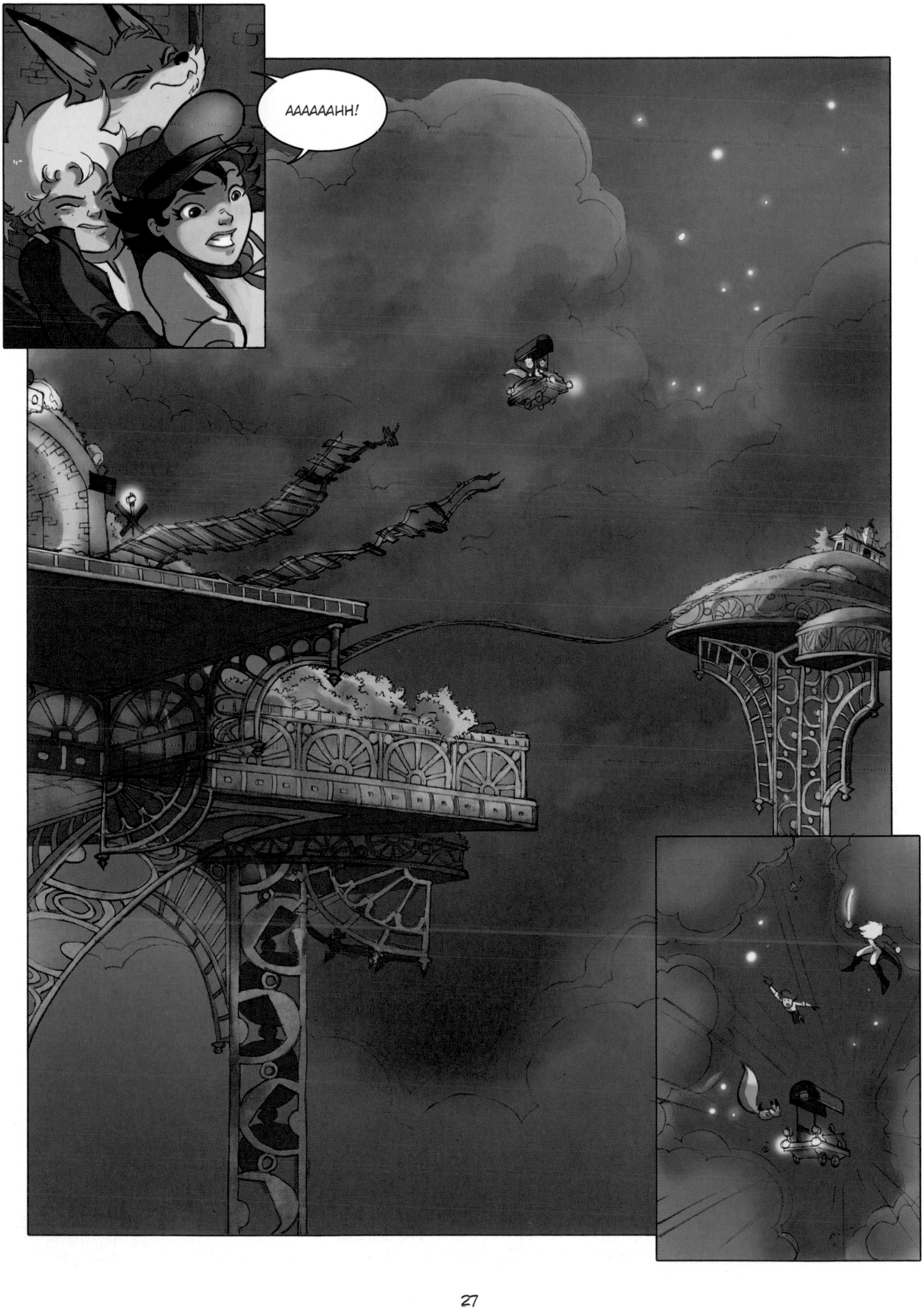
AAAAAAHH!

COME ON, FOX, I NEED YOUR HELP...

ROOM SERVICE? I'D LIKE A CHICKEN LEG WITH MASHED POTATOES...MAKE THAT TWO CHICKEN LEGS...

HUH? I'M NOT IN A HOTEL?

PLEASE, FOX! I'M LOSING MY GRIP...

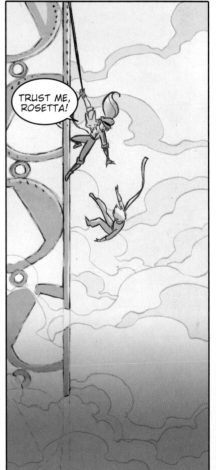

TRUST ME, ROSETTA!

LITTLE PRINCE! WAKE UP!

LET HIM GO. HE CAN TAKE CARE OF HIMSELF. THIS IS NO TIME FOR A NAP!

WHAT'S GOTTEN INTO YOU, FOX? I CAN'T JUST LET HIM FALL...

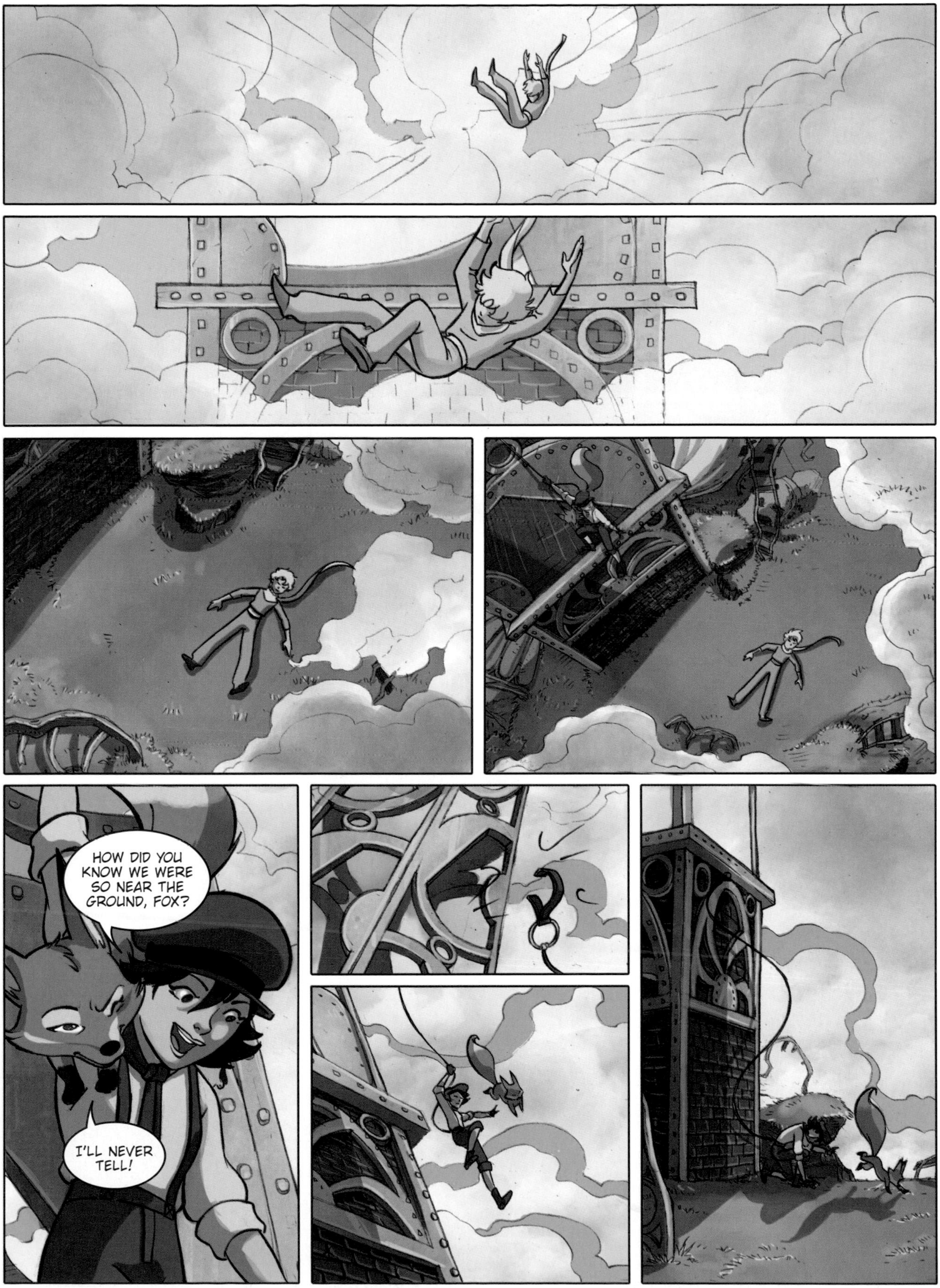
HOW DID YOU KNOW WE WERE SO NEAR THE GROUND, FOX?
I'LL NEVER TELL!

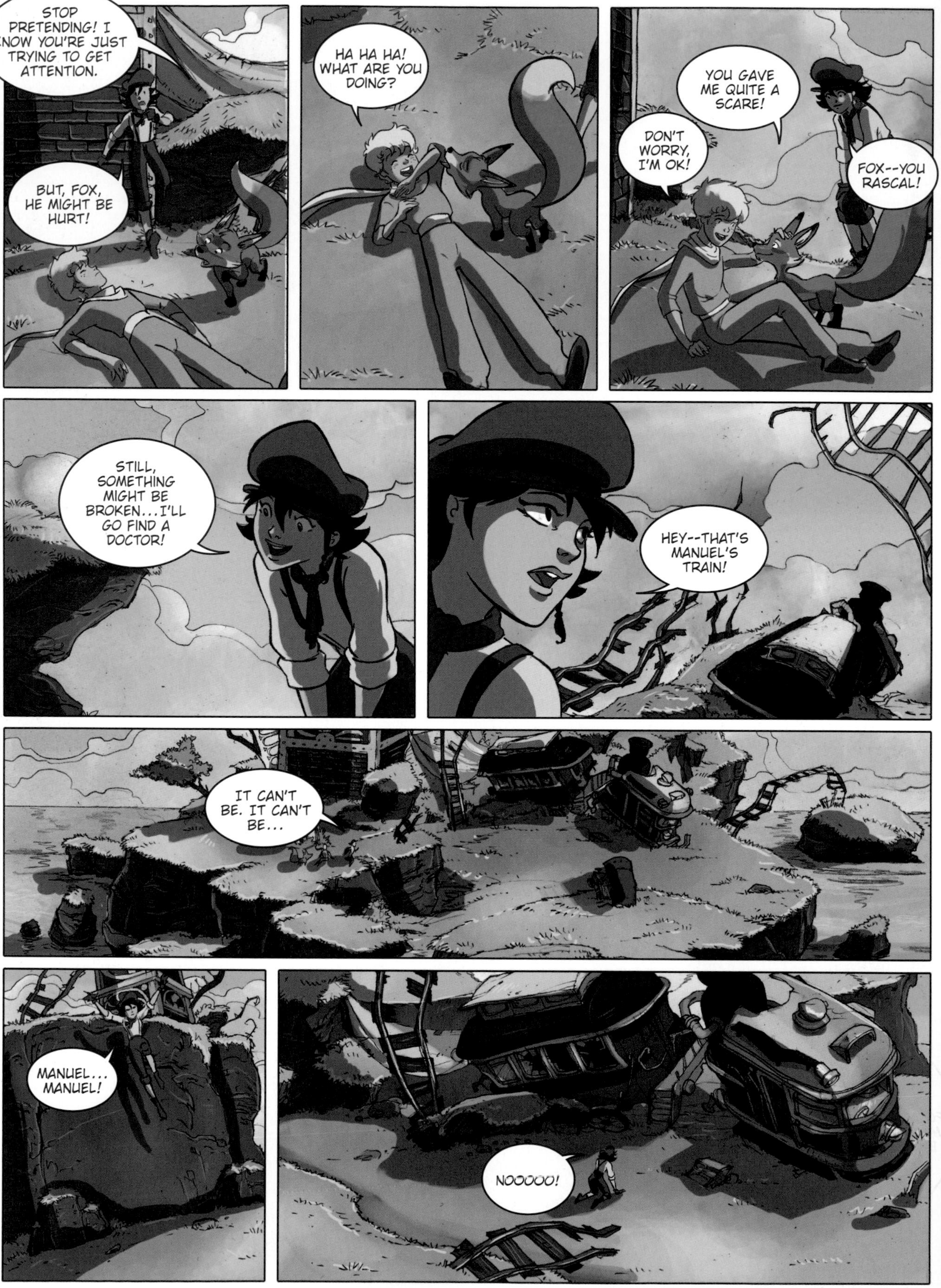
STOP PRETENDING! I KNOW YOU'RE JUST TRYING TO GET ATTENTION.
BUT, FOX, HE MIGHT BE HURT!
HA HA HA! WHAT ARE YOU DOING?
YOU GAVE ME QUITE A SCARE!
DON'T WORRY, I'M OK!
FOX--YOU RASCAL!
STILL, SOMETHING MIGHT BE BROKEN...I'LL GO FIND A DOCTOR!
HEY--THAT'S MANUEL'S TRAIN!
IT CAN'T BE. IT CAN'T BE...
MANUEL... MANUEL!
NOOOOO!

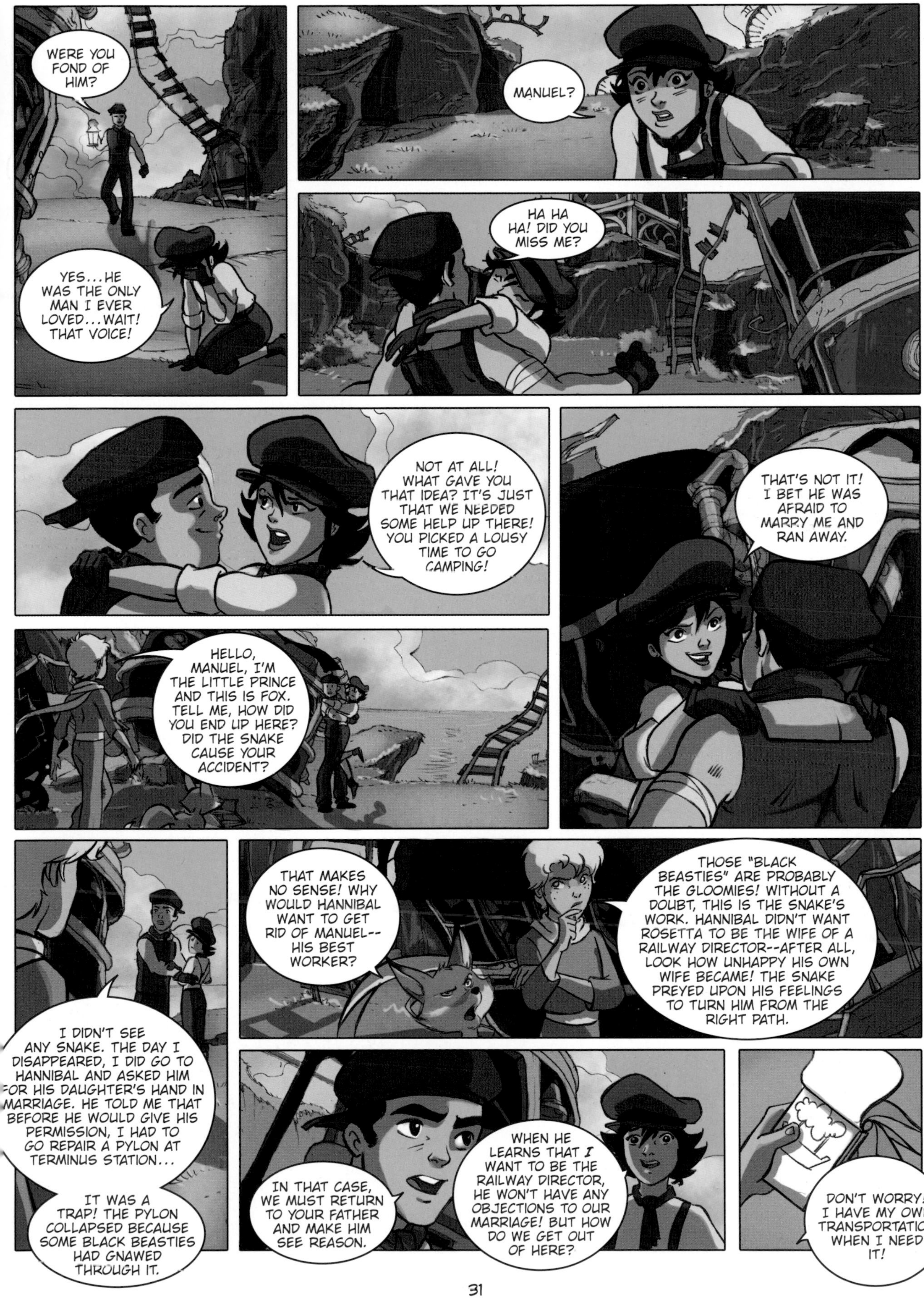
WERE YOU FOND OF HIM?
YES...HE WAS THE ONLY MAN I EVER LOVED...WAIT! THAT VOICE!
MANUEL?
HA HA HA! DID YOU MISS ME?
NOT AT ALL! WHAT GAVE YOU THAT IDEA? IT'S JUST THAT WE NEEDED SOME HELP UP THERE! YOU PICKED A LOUSY TIME TO GO CAMPING!
THAT'S NOT IT! I BET HE WAS AFRAID TO MARRY ME AND RAN AWAY.
HELLO, MANUEL, I'M THE LITTLE PRINCE AND THIS IS FOX. TELL ME, HOW DID YOU END UP HERE? DID THE SNAKE CAUSE YOUR ACCIDENT?
I DIDN'T SEE ANY SNAKE. THE DAY I DISAPPEARED, I DID GO TO HANNIBAL AND ASKED HIM FOR HIS DAUGHTER'S HAND IN MARRIAGE. HE TOLD ME THAT BEFORE HE WOULD GIVE HIS PERMISSION, I HAD TO GO REPAIR A PYLON AT TERMINUS STATION...
IT WAS A TRAP! THE PYLON COLLAPSED BECAUSE SOME BLACK BEASTIES HAD GNAWED THROUGH IT.
THAT MAKES NO SENSE! WHY WOULD HANNIBAL WANT TO GET RID OF MANUEL--HIS BEST WORKER?
THOSE "BLACK BEASTIES" ARE PROBABLY THE GLOOMIES! WITHOUT A DOUBT, THIS IS THE SNAKE'S WORK. HANNIBAL DIDN'T WANT ROSETTA TO BE THE WIFE OF A RAILWAY DIRECTOR--AFTER ALL, LOOK HOW UNHAPPY HIS OWN WIFE BECAME! THE SNAKE PREYED UPON HIS FEELINGS TO TURN HIM FROM THE RIGHT PATH.
IN THAT CASE, WE MUST RETURN TO YOUR FATHER AND MAKE HIM SEE REASON.
WHEN HE LEARNS THAT I WANT TO BE THE RAILWAY DIRECTOR, HE WON'T HAVE ANY OBJECTIONS TO OUR MARRIAGE! BUT HOW DO WE GET OUT OF HERE?
DON'T WORRY! I HAVE MY OWN TRANSPORTATION WHEN I NEED IT!

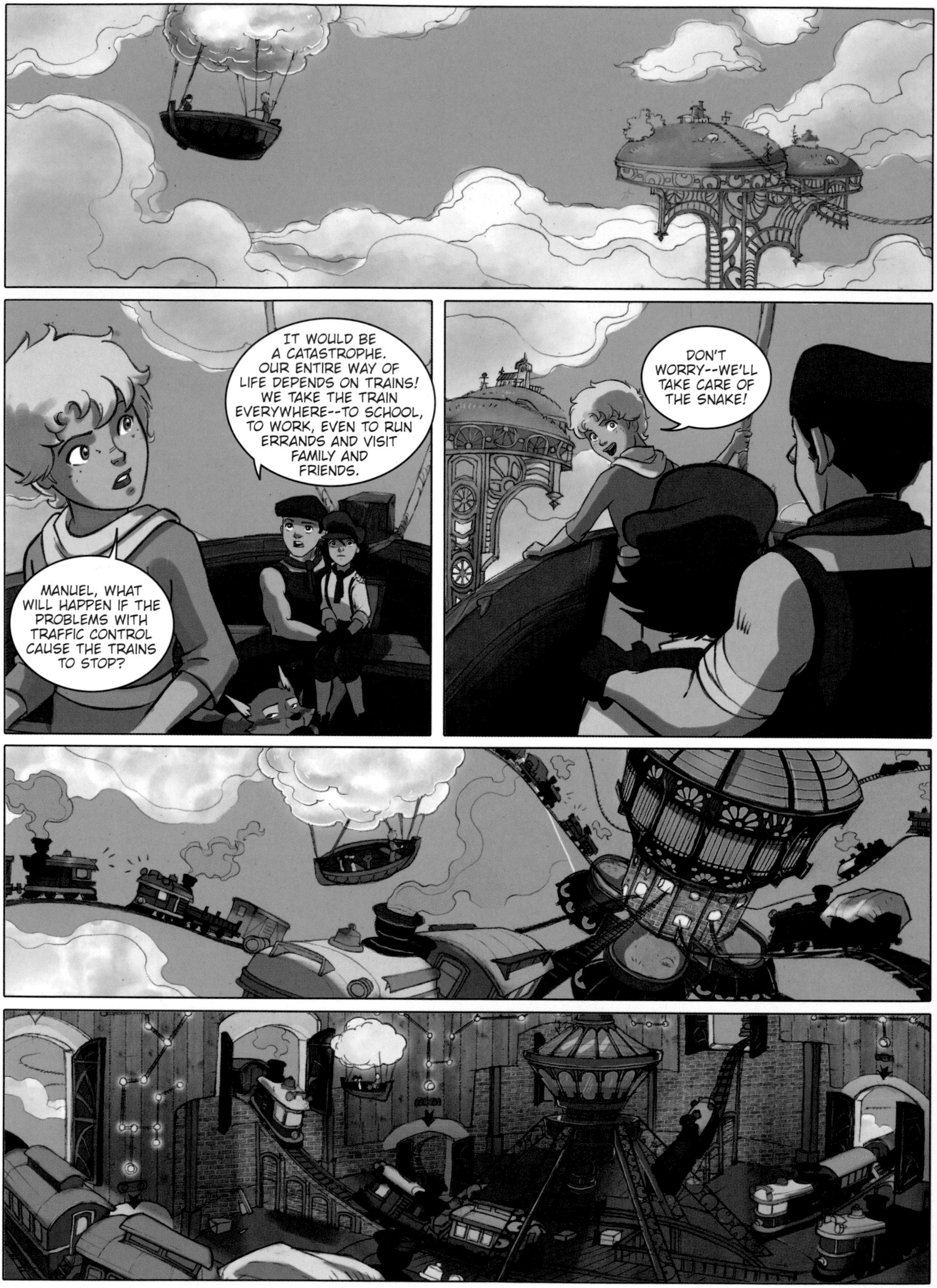
MANUEL, WHAT WILL HAPPEN IF THE PROBLEMS WITH TRAFFIC CONTROL CAUSE THE TRAINS TO STOP?
IT WOULD BE A CATASTROPHE. OUR ENTIRE WAY OF LIFE DEPENDS ON TRAINS! WE TAKE THE TRAIN EVERYWHERE--TO SCHOOL, TO WORK, EVEN TO RUN ERRANDS AND VISIT FAMILY AND FRIENDS.
DON'T WORRY--WE'LL TAKE CARE OF THE SNAKE!

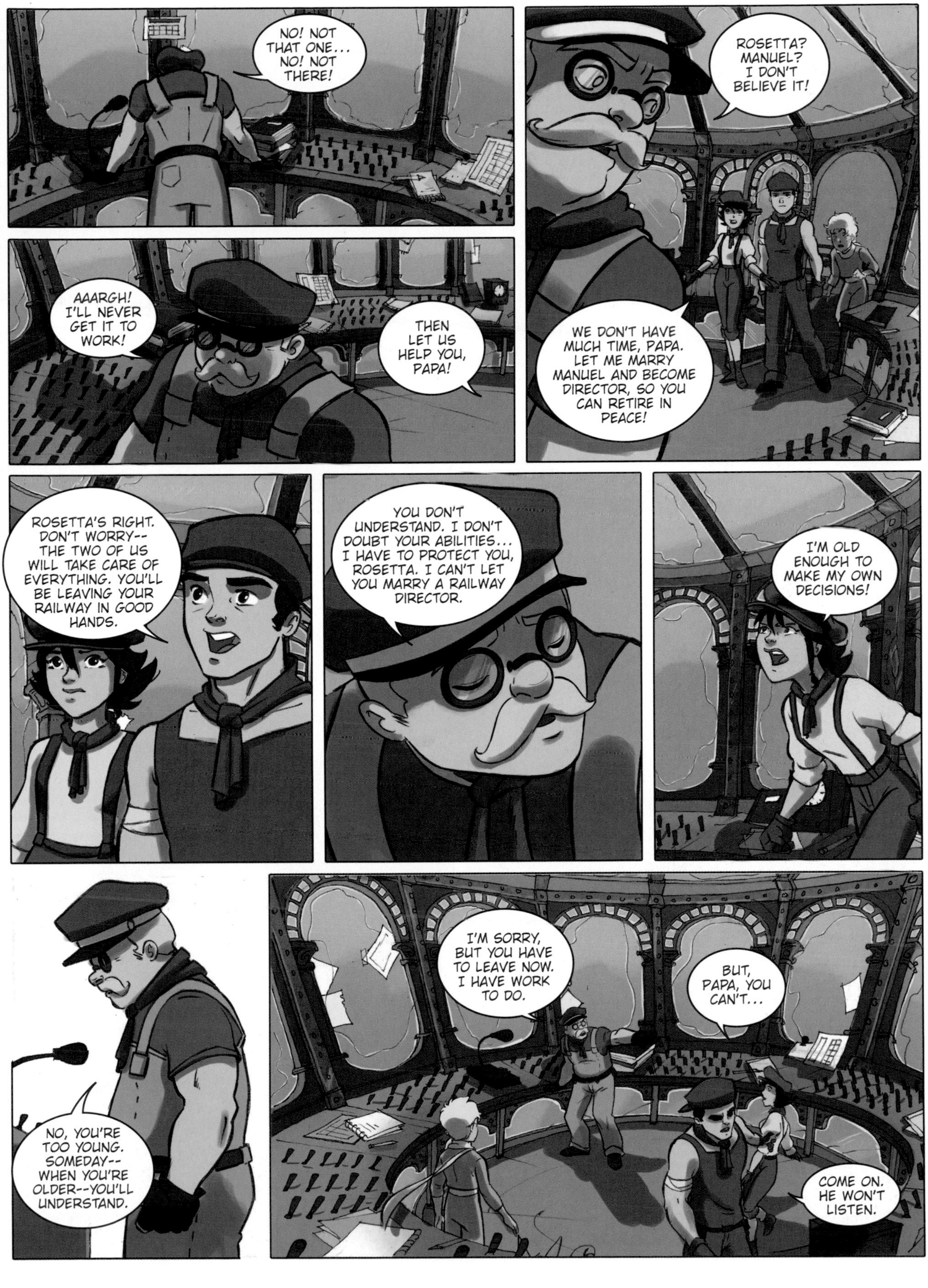
NO! NOT THAT ONE... NO! NOT THERE!
ROSETTA? MANUEL? I DON'T BELIEVE IT!
AAARGH! I'LL NEVER GET IT TO WORK!
THEN LET US HELP YOU, PAPA!
WE DON'T HAVE MUCH TIME, PAPA. LET ME MARRY MANUEL AND BECOME DIRECTOR, SO YOU CAN RETIRE IN PEACE!
ROSETTA'S RIGHT. DON'T WORRY-- THE TWO OF US WILL TAKE CARE OF EVERYTHING. YOU'LL BE LEAVING YOUR RAILWAY IN GOOD HANDS.
YOU DON'T UNDERSTAND. I DON'T DOUBT YOUR ABILITIES... I HAVE TO PROTECT YOU, ROSETTA. I CAN'T LET YOU MARRY A RAILWAY DIRECTOR.
I'M OLD ENOUGH TO MAKE MY OWN DECISIONS!
NO, YOU'RE TOO YOUNG. SOMEDAY-- WHEN YOU'RE OLDER--YOU'LL UNDERSTAND.
I'M SORRY, BUT YOU HAVE TO LEAVE NOW. I HAVE WORK TO DO.
BUT, PAPA, YOU CAN'T...
COME ON. HE WON'T LISTEN.

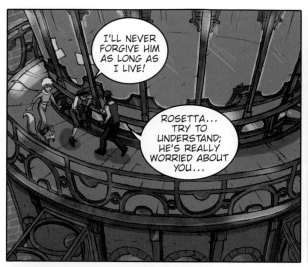

I'LL NEVER FORGIVE HIM AS LONG AS I LIVE!

ROSETTA... TRY TO UNDERSTAND; HE'S REALLY WORRIED ABOUT YOU...

SO NOW YOU'RE ON HIS SIDE?

THE LITTLE PRINCE SAYS THAT HE'S NOT RESPONSIBLE.

SO--IT'S ALL SOME *SNAKE'S* FAULT THAT MY FATHER DOESN'T CARE WHAT I WANT, JUST LIKE HE NEVER CARED WHAT MY MOTHER WANTED!

HEY! DON'T BLAME US FOR YOUR FAMILY'S PROBLEMS.

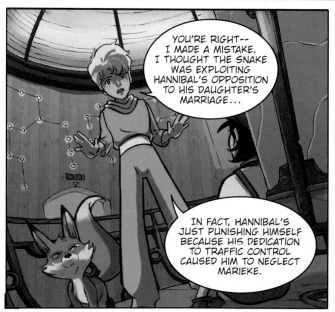

YOU'RE RIGHT-- I MADE A MISTAKE. I THOUGHT THE SNAKE WAS EXPLOITING HANNIBAL'S OPPOSITION TO HIS DAUGHTER'S MARRIAGE...

IN FACT, HANNIBAL'S JUST PUNISHING HIMSELF BECAUSE HIS DEDICATION TO TRAFFIC CONTROL CAUSED HIM TO NEGLECT MARIEKE.

OK, I DIDN'T UNDERSTAND ANY OF THAT.

WE NEED TO GO SEE MARIEKE RIGHT AWAY. SHE'S THE ONLY ONE WHO CAN HELP US!

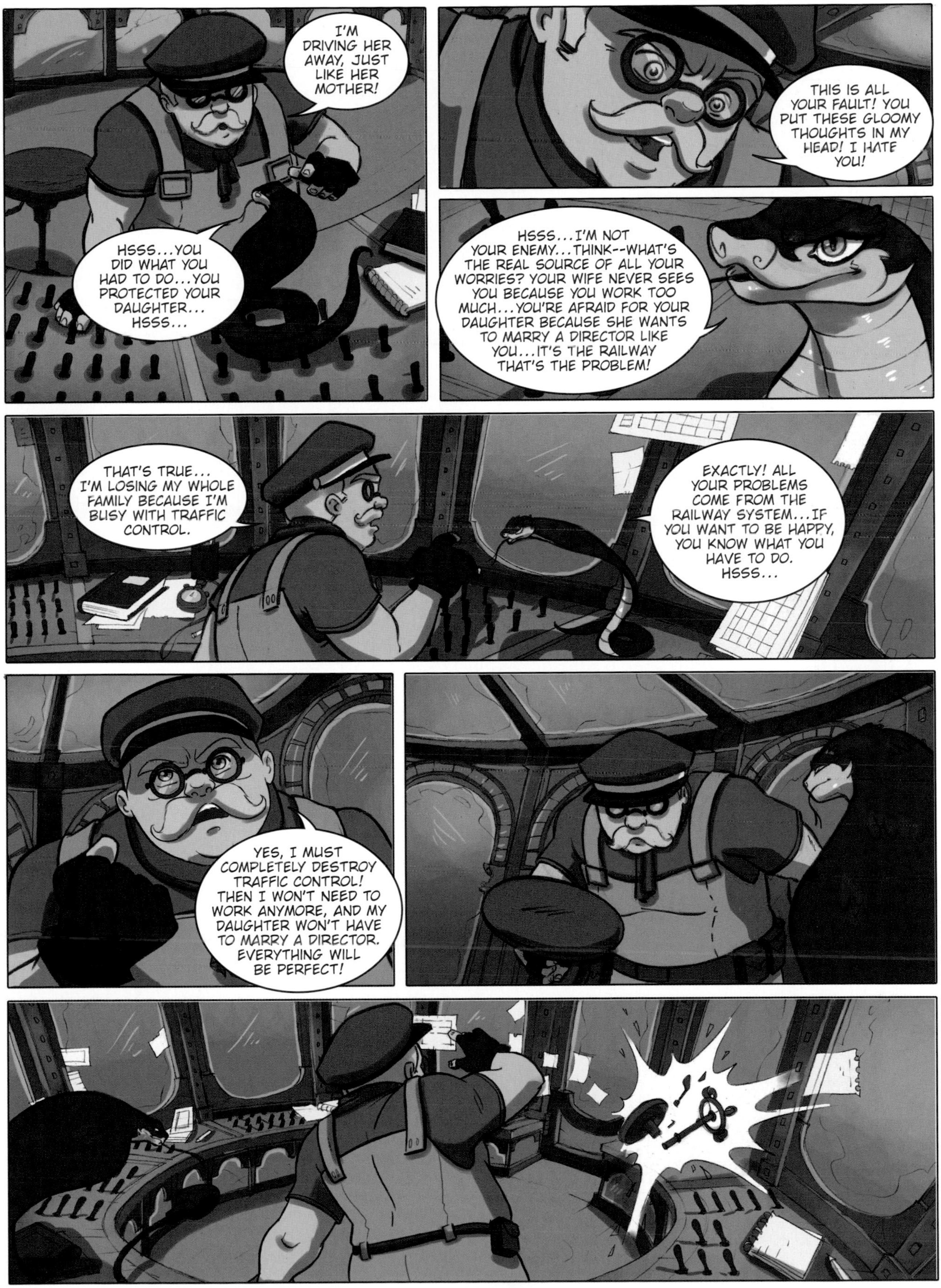
I'M DRIVING HER AWAY, JUST LIKE HER MOTHER!
HSSS...YOU DID WHAT YOU HAD TO DO...YOU PROTECTED YOUR DAUGHTER... HSSS...
THIS IS ALL YOUR FAULT! YOU PUT THESE GLOOMY THOUGHTS IN MY HEAD! I HATE YOU!
HSSS...I'M NOT YOUR ENEMY...THINK--WHAT'S THE REAL SOURCE OF ALL YOUR WORRIES? YOUR WIFE NEVER SEES YOU BECAUSE YOU WORK TOO MUCH...YOU'RE AFRAID FOR YOUR DAUGHTER BECAUSE SHE WANTS TO MARRY A DIRECTOR LIKE YOU...IT'S THE RAILWAY THAT'S THE PROBLEM!
THAT'S TRUE... I'M LOSING MY WHOLE FAMILY BECAUSE I'M BUSY WITH TRAFFIC CONTROL.
EXACTLY! ALL YOUR PROBLEMS COME FROM THE RAILWAY SYSTEM...IF YOU WANT TO BE HAPPY, YOU KNOW WHAT YOU HAVE TO DO. HSSS...
YES, I MUST COMPLETELY DESTROY TRAFFIC CONTROL! THEN I WON'T NEED TO WORK ANYMORE, AND MY DAUGHTER WON'T HAVE TO MARRY A DIRECTOR. EVERYTHING WILL BE PERFECT!

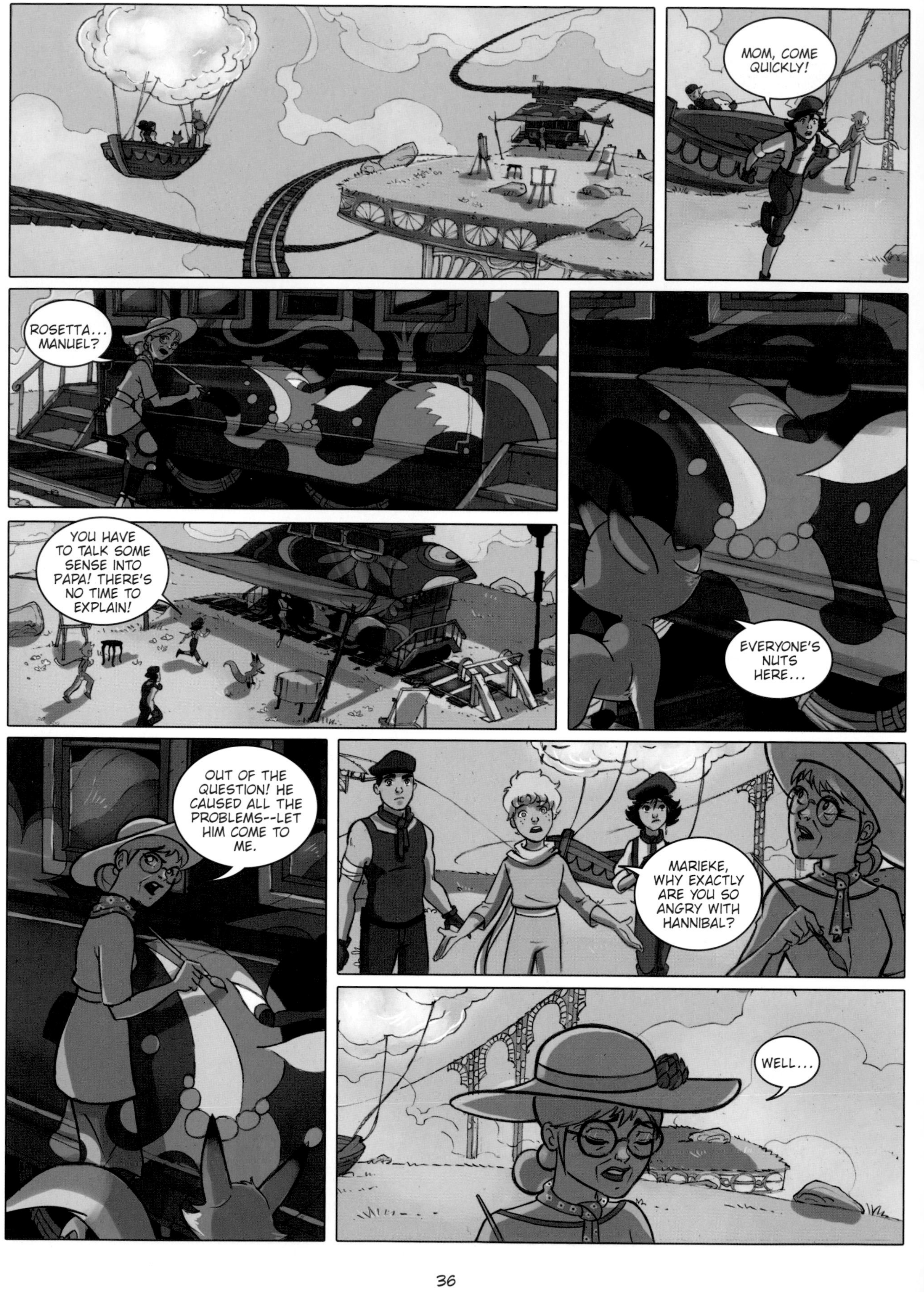
MOM, COME QUICKLY!
ROSETTA... MANUEL?
YOU HAVE TO TALK SOME SENSE INTO PAPA! THERE'S NO TIME TO EXPLAIN!
EVERYONE'S NUTS HERE...
OUT OF THE QUESTION! HE CAUSED ALL THE PROBLEMS--LET HIM COME TO ME.
MARIEKE, WHY EXACTLY ARE YOU SO ANGRY WITH HANNIBAL?
WELL...

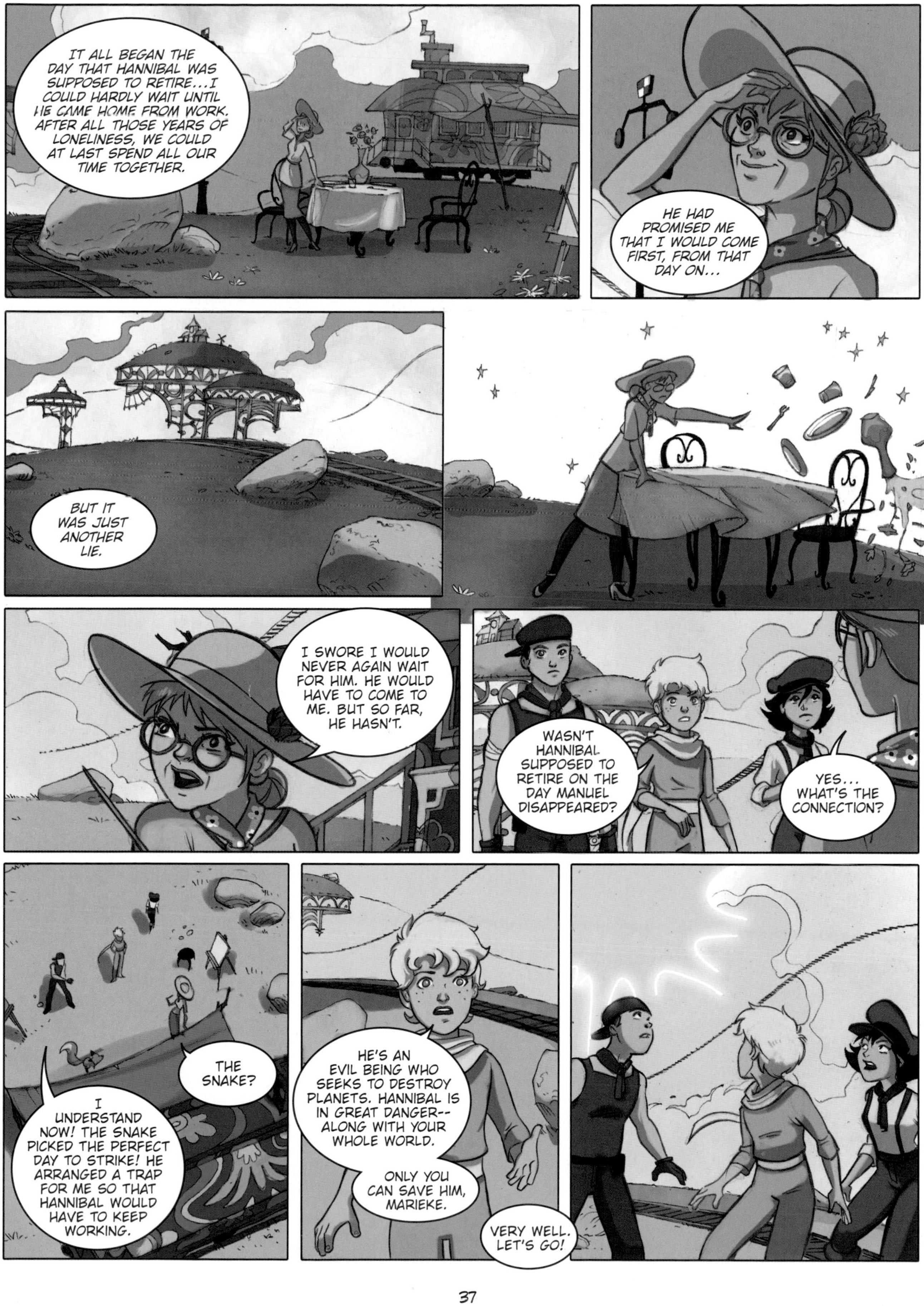
IT ALL BEGAN THE DAY THAT HANNIBAL WAS SUPPOSED TO RETIRE...I COULD HARDLY WAIT UNTIL HE CAME HOME FROM WORK. AFTER ALL THOSE YEARS OF LONELINESS, WE COULD AT LAST SPEND ALL OUR TIME TOGETHER.
HE HAD PROMISED ME THAT I WOULD COME FIRST, FROM THAT DAY ON...
BUT IT WAS JUST ANOTHER LIE.
I SWORE I WOULD NEVER AGAIN WAIT FOR HIM. HE WOULD HAVE TO COME TO ME. BUT SO FAR, HE HASN'T.
WASN'T HANNIBAL SUPPOSED TO RETIRE ON THE DAY MANUEL DISAPPEARED?
YES... WHAT'S THE CONNECTION?
THE SNAKE?
I UNDERSTAND NOW! THE SNAKE PICKED THE PERFECT DAY TO STRIKE! HE ARRANGED A TRAP FOR ME SO THAT HANNIBAL WOULD HAVE TO KEEP WORKING.
HE'S AN EVIL BEING WHO SEEKS TO DESTROY PLANETS. HANNIBAL IS IN GREAT DANGER-- ALONG WITH YOUR WHOLE WORLD.
ONLY YOU CAN SAVE HIM, MARIEKE.
VERY WELL. LET'S GO!

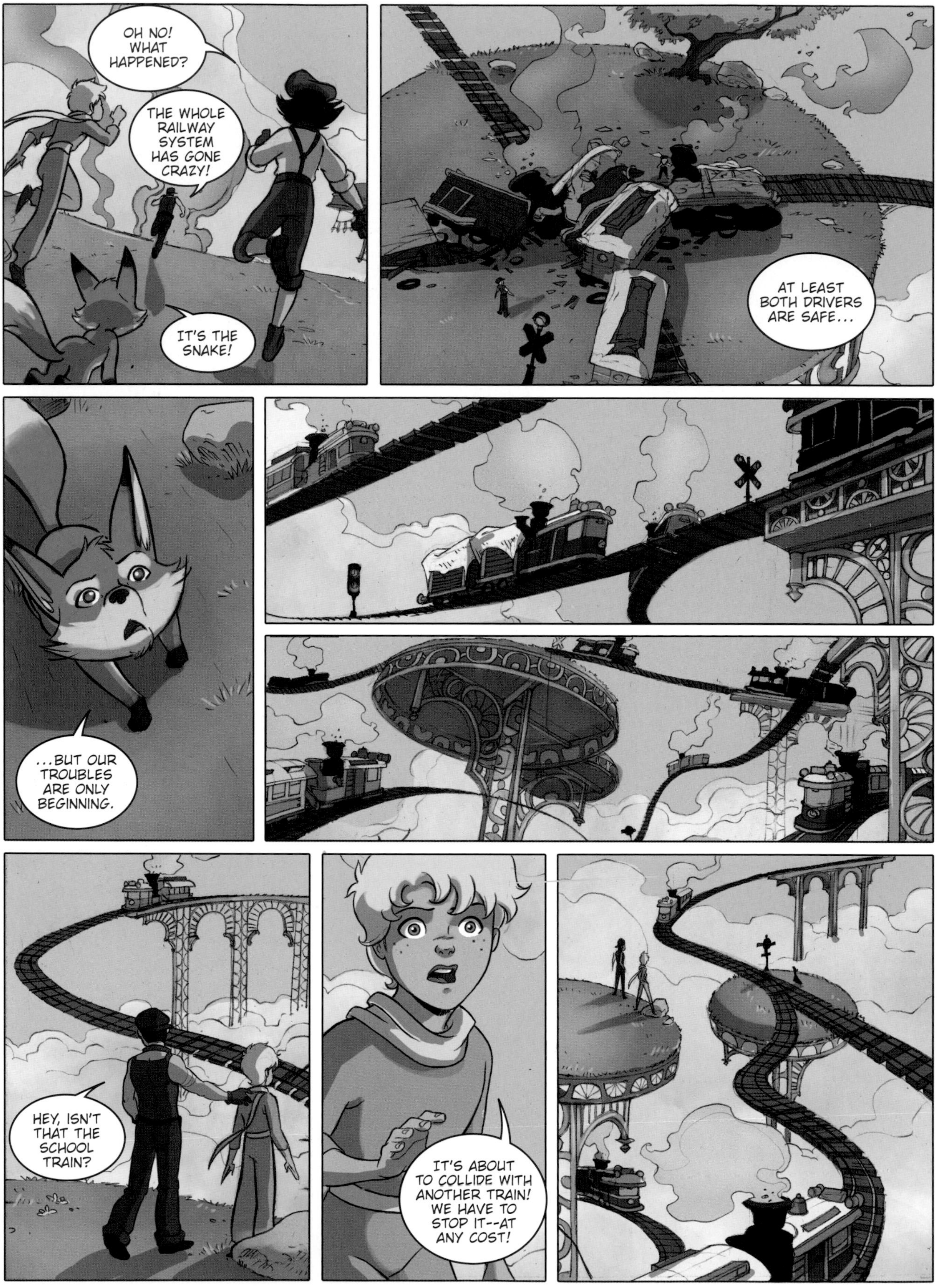
OH NO! WHAT HAPPENED?
THE WHOLE RAILWAY SYSTEM HAS GONE CRAZY!
IT'S THE SNAKE!
AT LEAST BOTH DRIVERS ARE SAFE...
...BUT OUR TROUBLES ARE ONLY BEGINNING.
HEY, ISN'T THAT THE SCHOOL TRAIN?
IT'S ABOUT TO COLLIDE WITH ANOTHER TRAIN! WE HAVE TO STOP IT--AT ANY COST!

I'LL TAKE CARE OF IT!

LET US DO IT, LITTLE PRINCE. IT'S OUR JOB!

BE CAREFUL!

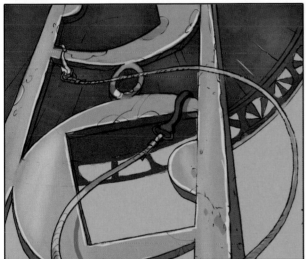

THEY'LL DO FINE. IT'S UP TO US TO CONVINCE HANNIBAL TO STOP THIS MADNESS!

HOW MARVELOUS-- A GIANT FLYING SQUIRREL!

TO TRAFFIC CONTROL!

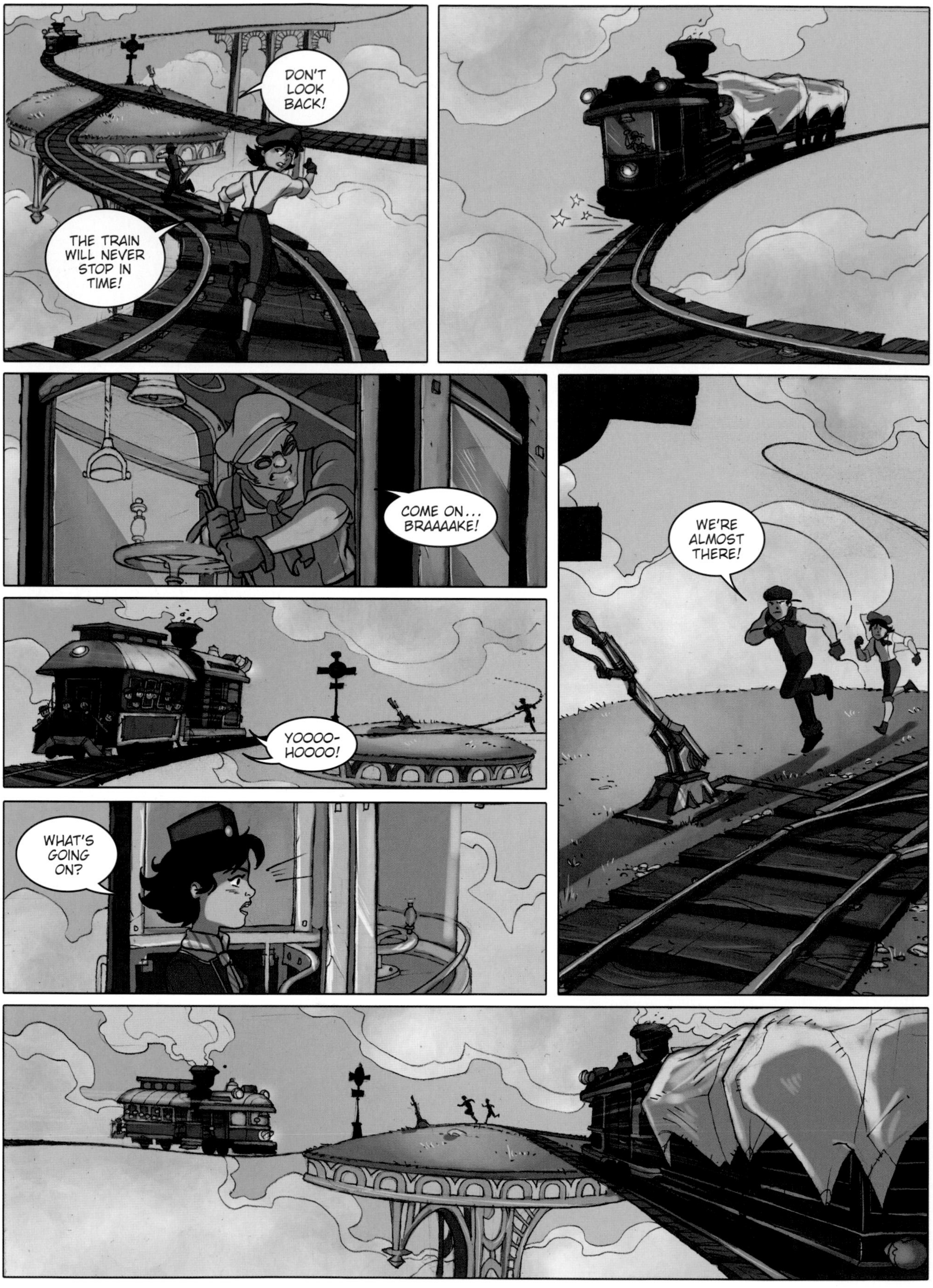
DON'T LOOK BACK!
THE TRAIN WILL NEVER STOP IN TIME!
COME ON... BRAAAAKE!
WE'RE ALMOST THERE!
YOOOO-HOOOO!
WHAT'S GOING ON?

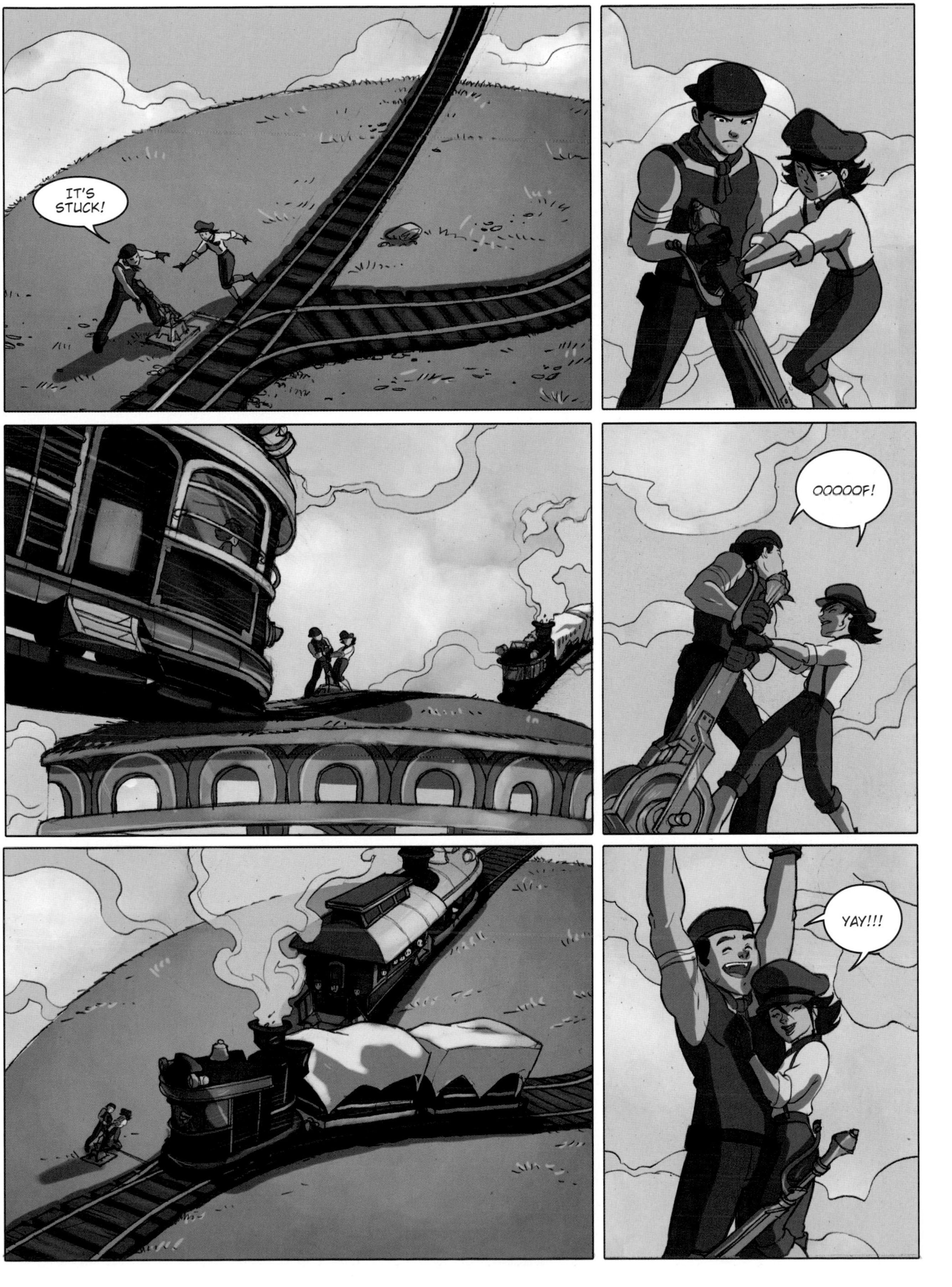
IT'S STUCK!
OOOOOF!
YAY!!!

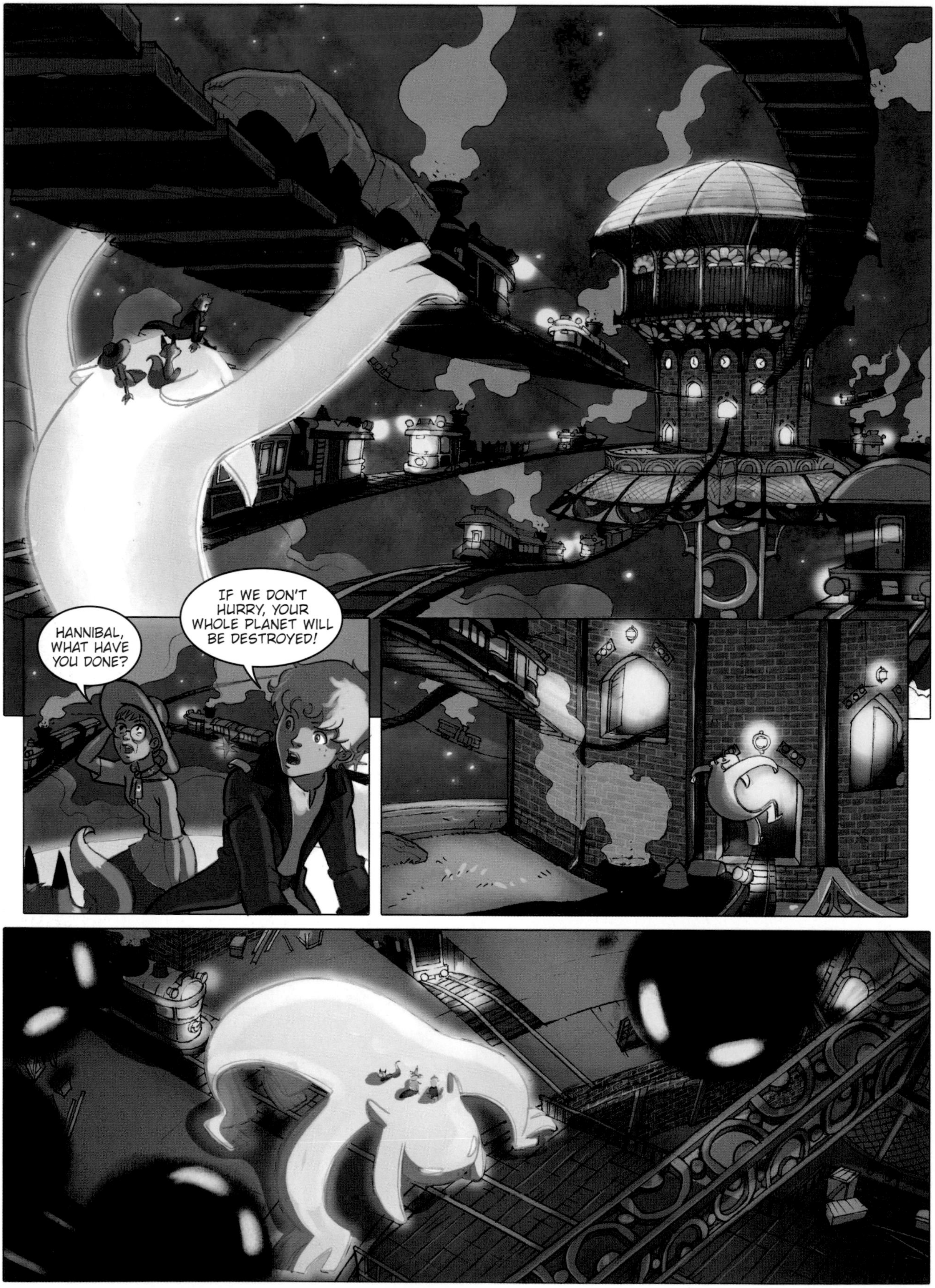
HANNIBAL, WHAT HAVE YOU DONE?
IF WE DON'T HURRY, YOUR WHOLE PLANET WILL BE DESTROYED!

THE
GLOOMIES!

GO FIND
HANNIBAL--
I'LL COVER
YOU!

WOW! I'D
LOVE TO
PAINT THESE
BLACK FLUFFY
THINGS!

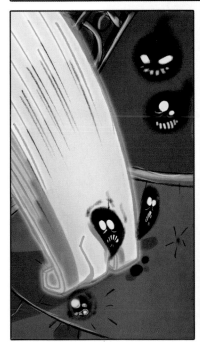

YOU
WON'T GET
BY ME!

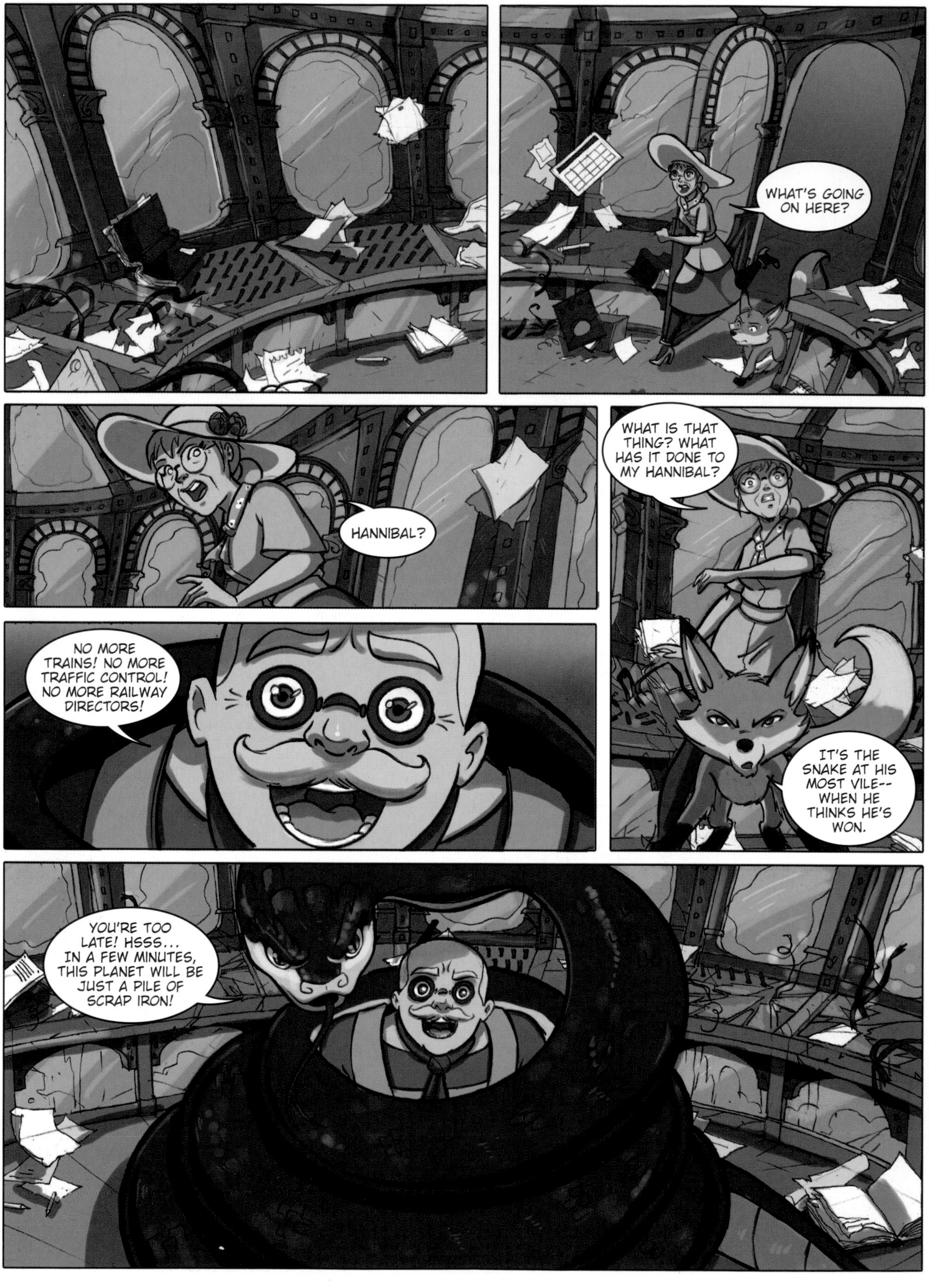

WHAT'S GOING ON HERE?
HANNIBAL?
WHAT IS THAT THING? WHAT HAS IT DONE TO MY HANNIBAL?
NO MORE TRAINS! NO MORE TRAFFIC CONTROL! NO MORE RAILWAY DIRECTORS!
IT'S THE SNAKE AT HIS MOST VILE-- WHEN HE THINKS HE'S WON.
YOU'RE TOO LATE! HSSS... IN A FEW MINUTES, THIS PLANET WILL BE JUST A PILE OF SCRAP IRON!

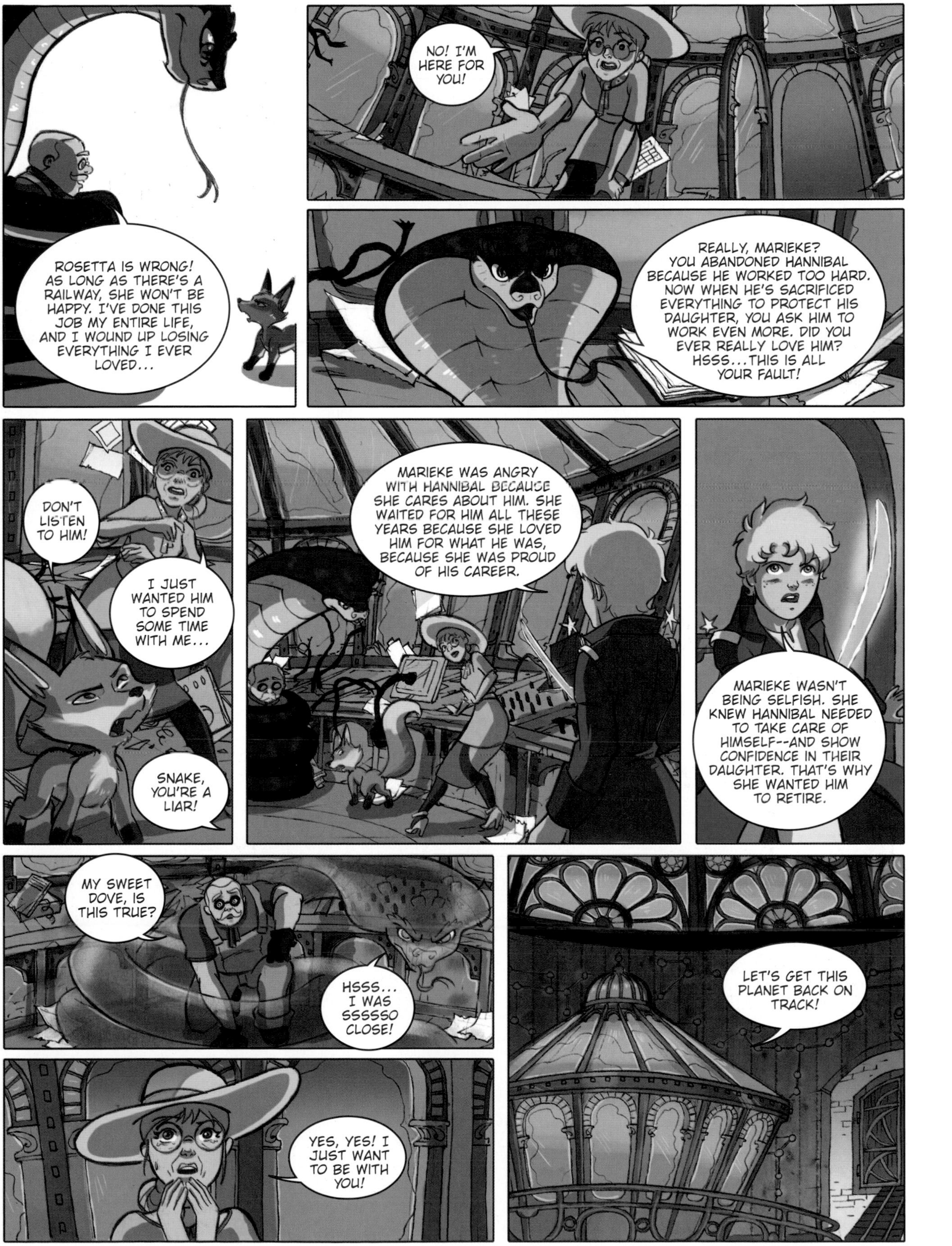
ROSETTA IS WRONG! AS LONG AS THERE'S A RAILWAY, SHE WON'T BE HAPPY. I'VE DONE THIS JOB MY ENTIRE LIFE, AND I WOUND UP LOSING EVERYTHING I EVER LOVED...
NO! I'M HERE FOR YOU!
REALLY, MARIEKE? YOU ABANDONED HANNIBAL BECAUSE HE WORKED TOO HARD. NOW WHEN HE'S SACRIFICED EVERYTHING TO PROTECT HIS DAUGHTER, YOU ASK HIM TO WORK EVEN MORE. DID YOU EVER REALLY LOVE HIM? HSSS...THIS IS ALL YOUR FAULT!
DON'T LISTEN TO HIM!
I JUST WANTED HIM TO SPEND SOME TIME WITH ME...
SNAKE, YOU'RE A LIAR!
MARIEKE WAS ANGRY WITH HANNIBAL BECAUSE SHE CARES ABOUT HIM. SHE WAITED FOR HIM ALL THESE YEARS BECAUSE SHE LOVED HIM FOR WHAT HE WAS, BECAUSE SHE WAS PROUD OF HIS CAREER.
MARIEKE WASN'T BEING SELFISH. SHE KNEW HANNIBAL NEEDED TO TAKE CARE OF HIMSELF--AND SHOW CONFIDENCE IN THEIR DAUGHTER. THAT'S WHY SHE WANTED HIM TO RETIRE.
MY SWEET DOVE, IS THIS TRUE?
HSSS... I WAS SSSSSO CLOSE!
YES, YES! I JUST WANT TO BE WITH YOU!
LET'S GET THIS PLANET BACK ON TRACK!

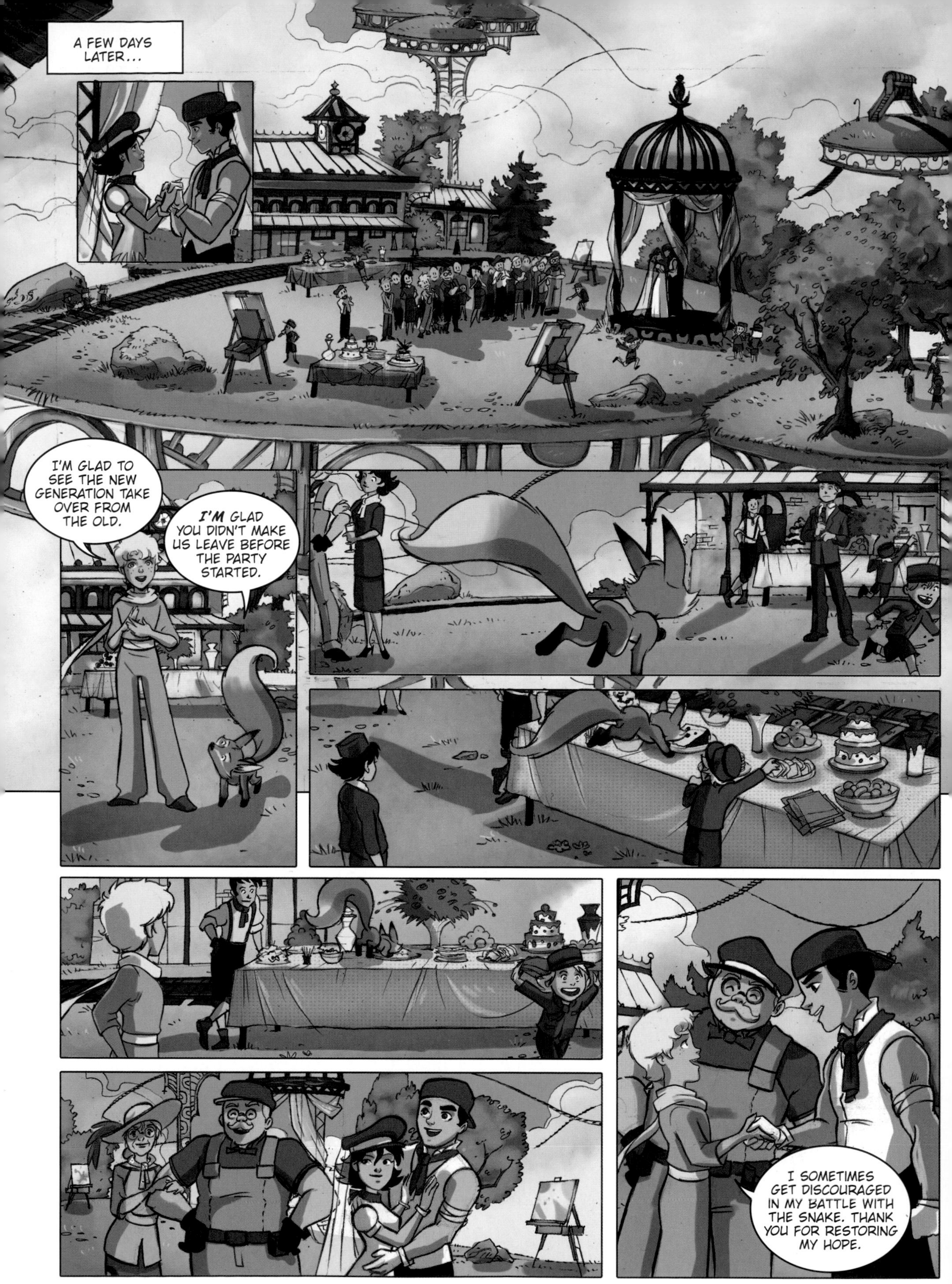
A FEW DAYS LATER...
I'M GLAD TO SEE THE NEW GENERATION TAKE OVER FROM THE OLD.
I'M GLAD YOU DIDN'T MAKE US LEAVE BEFORE THE PARTY STARTED.
I SOMETIMES GET DISCOURAGED IN MY BATTLE WITH THE SNAKE. THANK YOU FOR RESTORING MY HOPE.

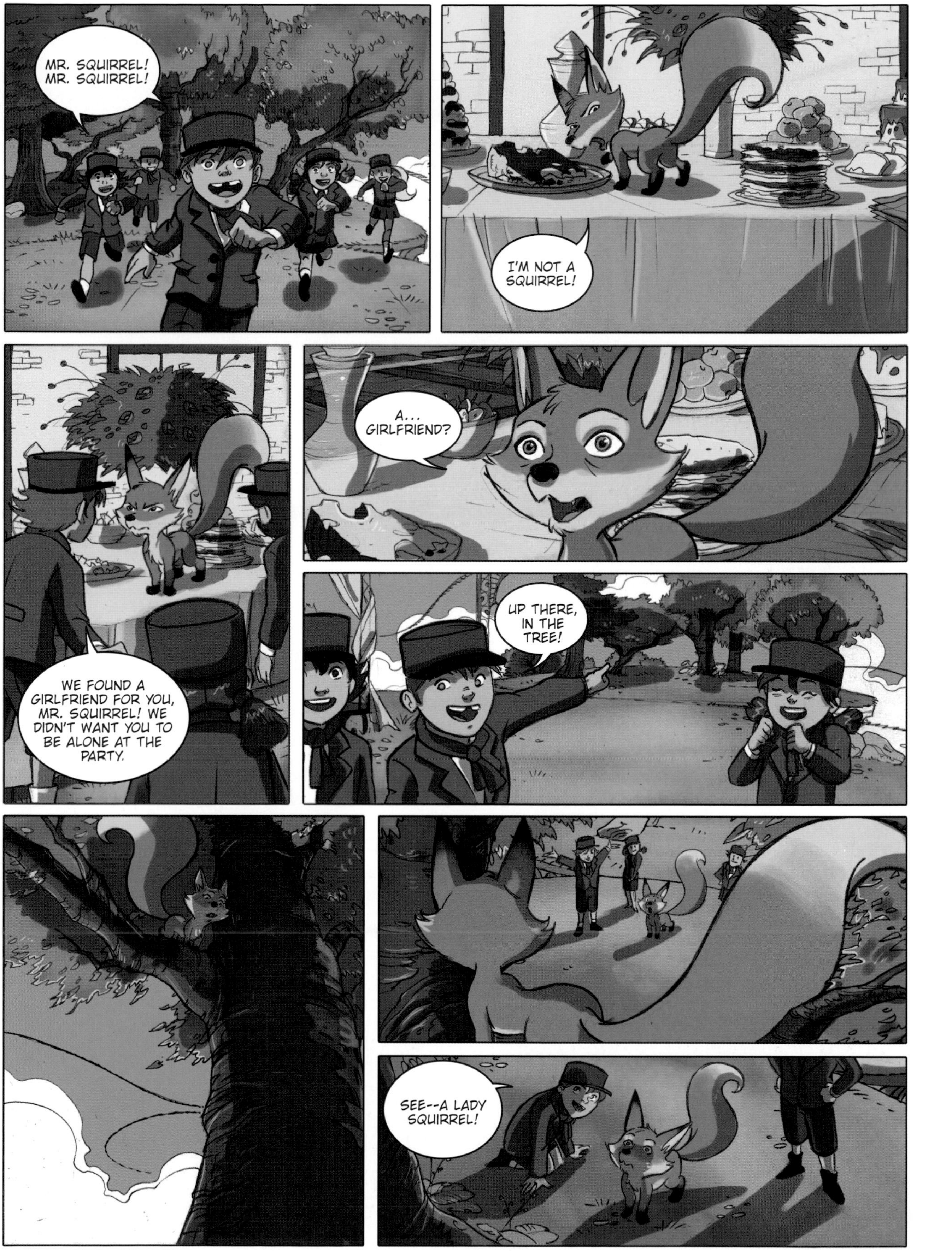
MR. SQUIRREL! MR. SQUIRREL!
I'M NOT A SQUIRREL!
WE FOUND A GIRLFRIEND FOR YOU, MR. SQUIRREL! WE DIDN'T WANT YOU TO BE ALONE AT THE PARTY.
A... GIRLFRIEND?
UP THERE, IN THE TREE!
SEE--A LADY SQUIRREL!

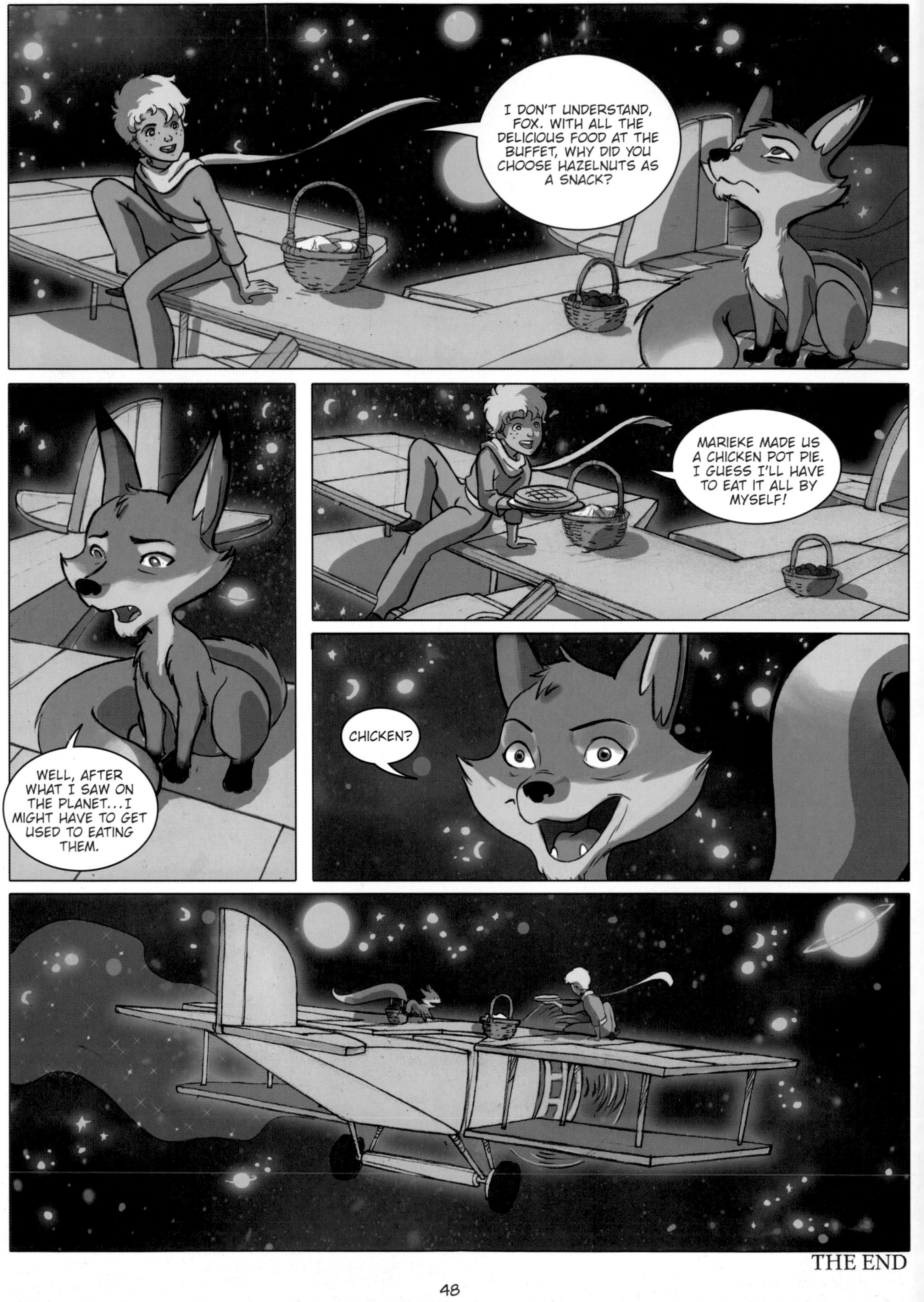
I DON'T UNDERSTAND, FOX. WITH ALL THE DELICIOUS FOOD AT THE BUFFET, WHY DID YOU CHOOSE HAZELNUTS AS A SNACK?
WELL, AFTER WHAT I SAW ON THE PLANET...I MIGHT HAVE TO GET USED TO EATING THEM.
MARIEKE MADE US A CHICKEN POT PIE. I GUESS I'LL HAVE TO EAT IT ALL BY MYSELF!
CHICKEN?

THE END

The Little Prince

AS IMAGINED BY

NICOLAS KÉRAMIDAS

COWRITER
MILO KÉRAMIDAS

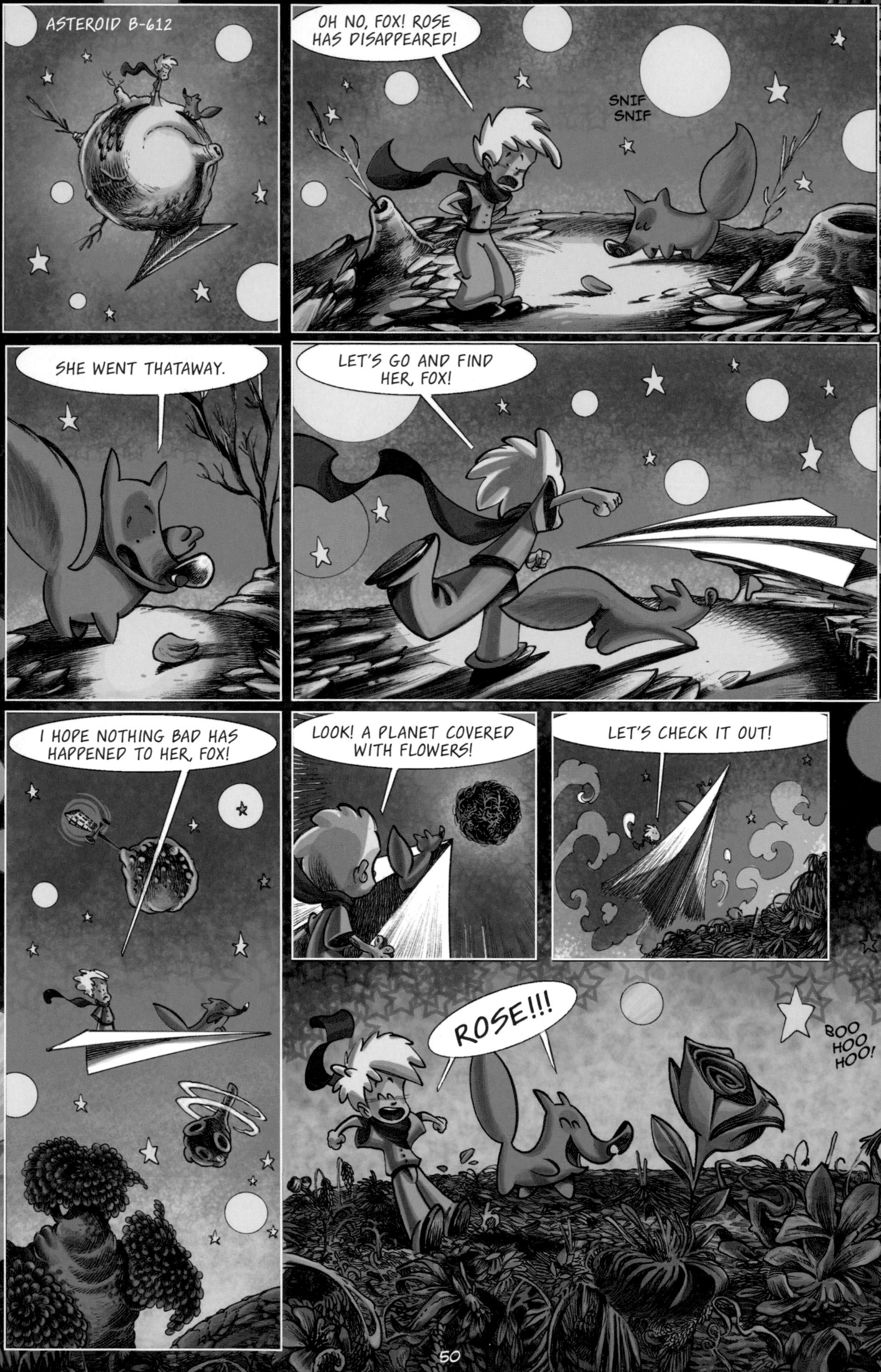
ASTEROID B-612
OH NO, FOX! ROSE HAS DISAPPEARED!
SNIF SNIF
SHE WENT THATAWAY.
LET'S GO AND FIND HER, FOX!
I HOPE NOTHING BAD HAS HAPPENED TO HER, FOX!
LOOK! A PLANET COVERED WITH FLOWERS!
LET'S CHECK IT OUT!
ROSE!!!
BOO HOO HOO!

WHERE'S THAT SOBBING COMING FROM?

BOO! HOO! THIS WHOLE TRAGEDY IS MY FAULT!

BUT...BUT WHY?

I USED TO BE THE BEST GARDENER IN THE GALAXY...

EVERYONE WANTED MY FLOWERS. I WORKED HARD SO THAT PEOPLE WOULD BE HAPPY!

THEN ALONG CAME PLASTIC. SOON EVERYONE WANTED PLASTIC FLOWERS, FLOWERS THAT WOULD NEVER WILT, FLOWERS THAT WOULD LAST FOREVER...

MY OWN FLOWERS BEGAN TO WILT. AS I SEARCHED FOR A CURE, I CAUGHT SIGHT OF YOUR ROSE...

PLEASE FORGIVE ME.

DON'T CRY, MR. GARDENER. FOX, ROSE, AND I ARE GOING TO HELP YOU!

SO THE LITTLE PRINCE, FOX, AND ROSE WENT TO FIND THEIR FRIEND THE CLOUD...

WHO, IN JUST A FEW HOURS, TRANSFORMED ALL THE WILTED FLOWERS...

...INTO A MAGNIFICENT GARDEN, EVEN MORE BEAUTIFUL THAN BEFORE. THE GARDENER FOUND HIS SMILE AGAIN, AND ROSE, HER FRIENDS...

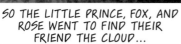

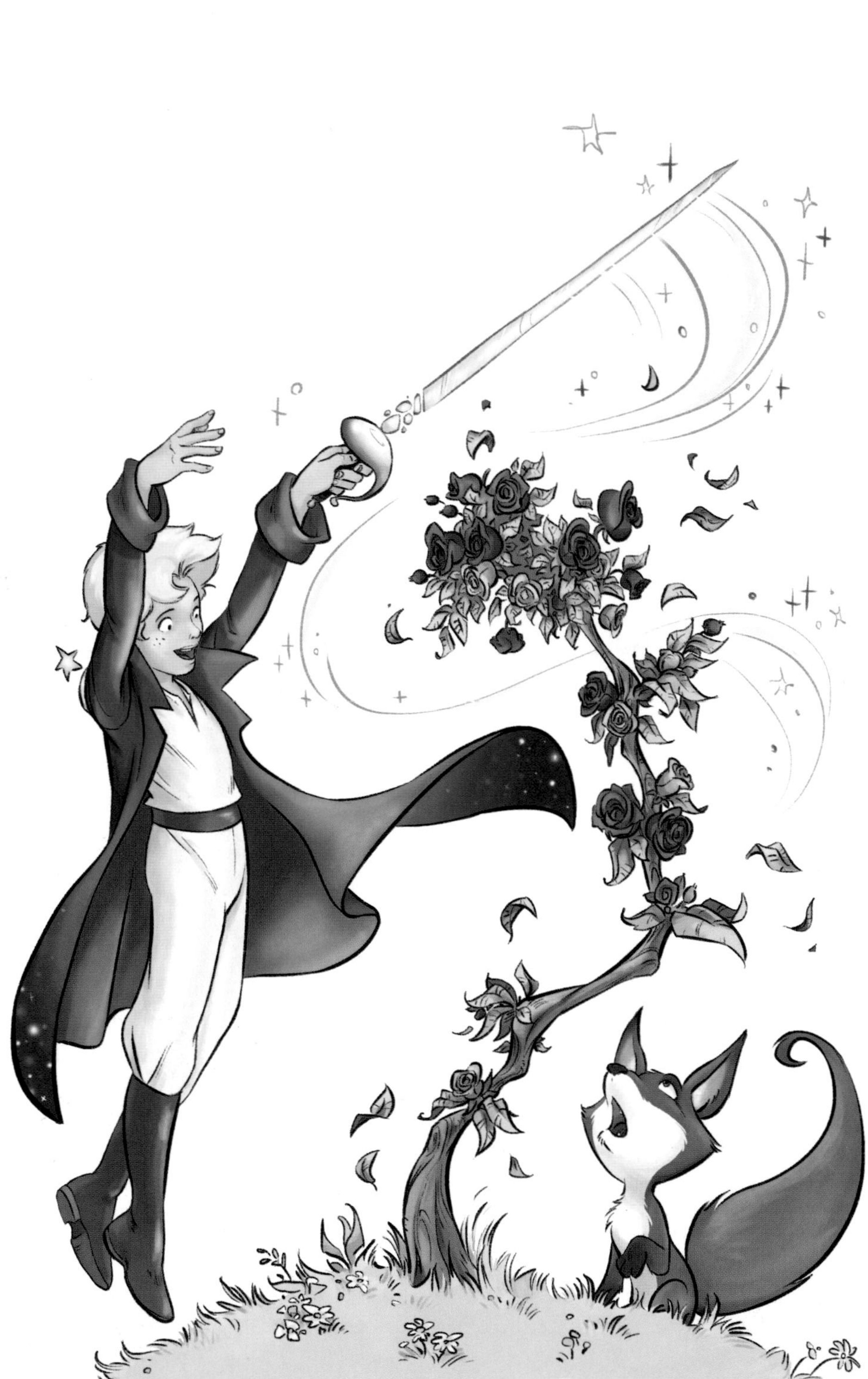

he finally began work on *The Little Prince*. The story is narrated by a pilot who has crashed his plane into the Sahara Desert. He meets a little prince visiting from a faraway asteroid. Along the way, the prince also meets Fox and Snake. By late 1942, after spending the spring and summer writing and illustrating, Saint-Exupéry had completed his novel, and in April 1943 it was published in his native language of French *(Le Petit Prince)* and in English.

Saint-Exupéry was eager to return to the war. He decided to join the Free French Forces in Algeria, who were continuing the fight against the Axis powers. Because of his age, at first he had a hard time convincing them to let him fly. He was authorized to fly five dangerous missions. In fact, he flew eight. On July 31, 1944, Saint-Exupéry went on a scouting flight to prepare for military landings in the south of France. His plane disappeared over the water, and he was never seen again.

Over the decades since *The Little Prince* was published, it has gone on to become one of the best-selling novels of all time. In 2003, a small moon in our solar system's asteroid belt was named Petit-Prince in honor of the masterpiece Saint-Exupéry created.

THE LITTLE PRINCE IN THE TWENTY-FIRST CENTURY

The Little Prince is a landmark of literature and one of the most translated and beloved books in the world. It tackles universal topics with a unique philosophical and poetic sensibility. Sixty-five years after the first edition, the Saint-Exupéry Estate decided to bring the character back for a whole new generation . . . and for everyone who has ever loved the boy who sees the world with his heart.

The Little Prince now returns in a series of new adventures that remain true to the spirit of the original work. He will travel from planet to planet chasing the wicked Snake, who wants to plunge the whole universe into darkness. On each planet, the Snake sends bad thoughts into the minds of its inhabitants, making them sad and grim, draining the life out of their planet. The Little Prince must leave his beautiful Rose behind and must use his vision and courage to defeat the Snake, bringing along his friend Fox to save planets in danger across the universe.

ABOUT THE ADAPTERS

After several years in video games and Japanese animation, adapter Guillaume Dorison became literary editor for the publisher Les Humanoïdes Associés in 2006, where he launched the Shogun Collection dedicated to original manga. In June 2010, he founded Élyum Studio with Didier Poli, Jean-Baptiste Hostache, and Xavier Dorison to provide services for the creation of graphic novels. In addition to his position as director of writing for Élyum Studio, he has more than two dozen comics and manga to his credit under the pseudonym IZU, has written several titles in the Explora series on world explorers for French publisher Glénat, and won the 2010 Animeland Prize for best French manga.

Didier Poli, artistic director for the new graphic novel adaptations based on *The Little Prince*, was born in Lyon in 1971. After graduate studies in applied arts, he worked for various animation studios including Disney. He was working as artistic director for the video game company Kalisto Entertainment when he met Manuel Bichebois in 2001 and began drawing Bichebois's graphic novel series L'Enfant de l'orage. At the 2004 Nîmes Festival, Didier Poli received the Bronze Boar prize for young talent. He continues, along with his work on graphic novels, to work regularly in cartoons and video games as a designer and storyboard artist.

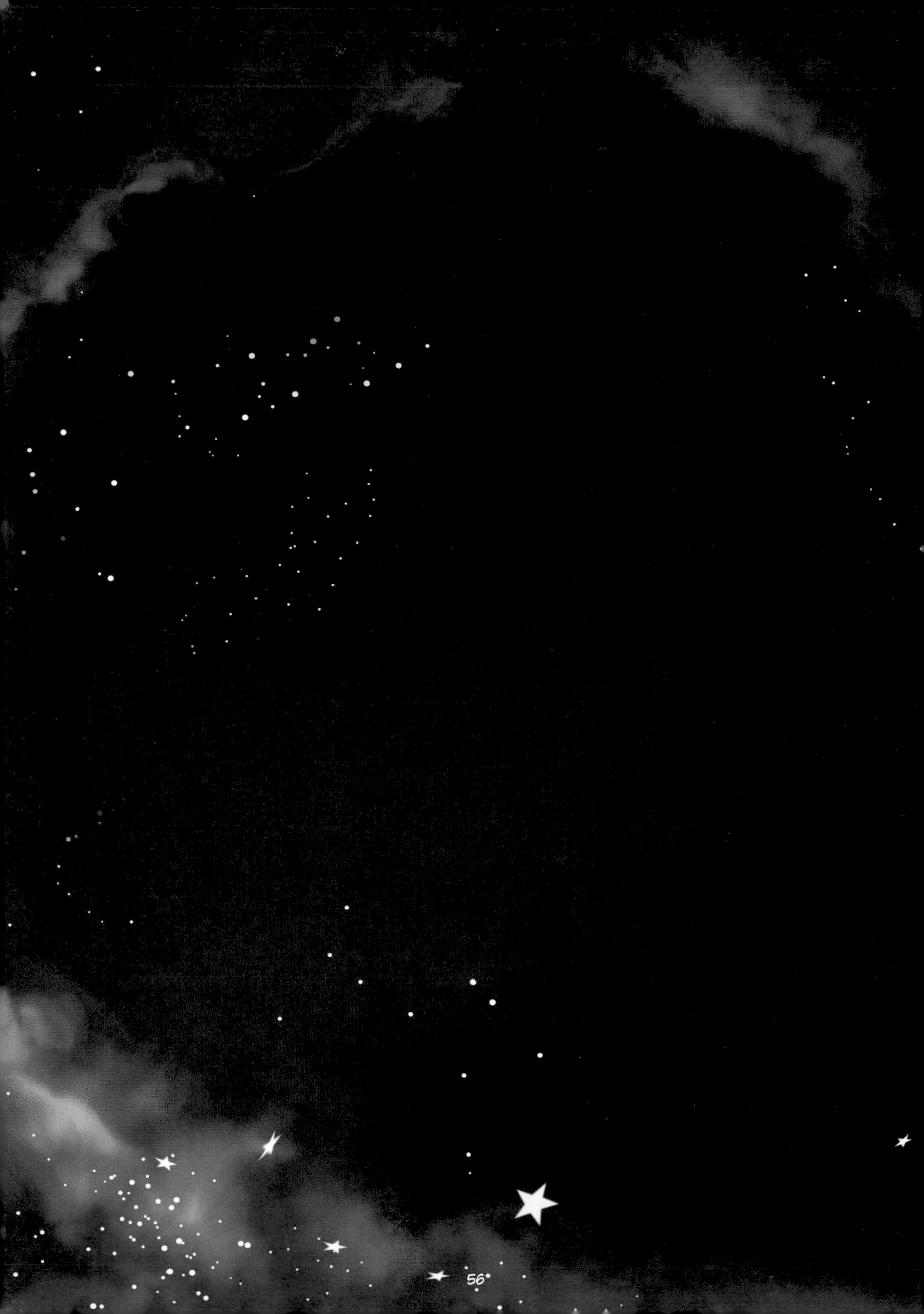

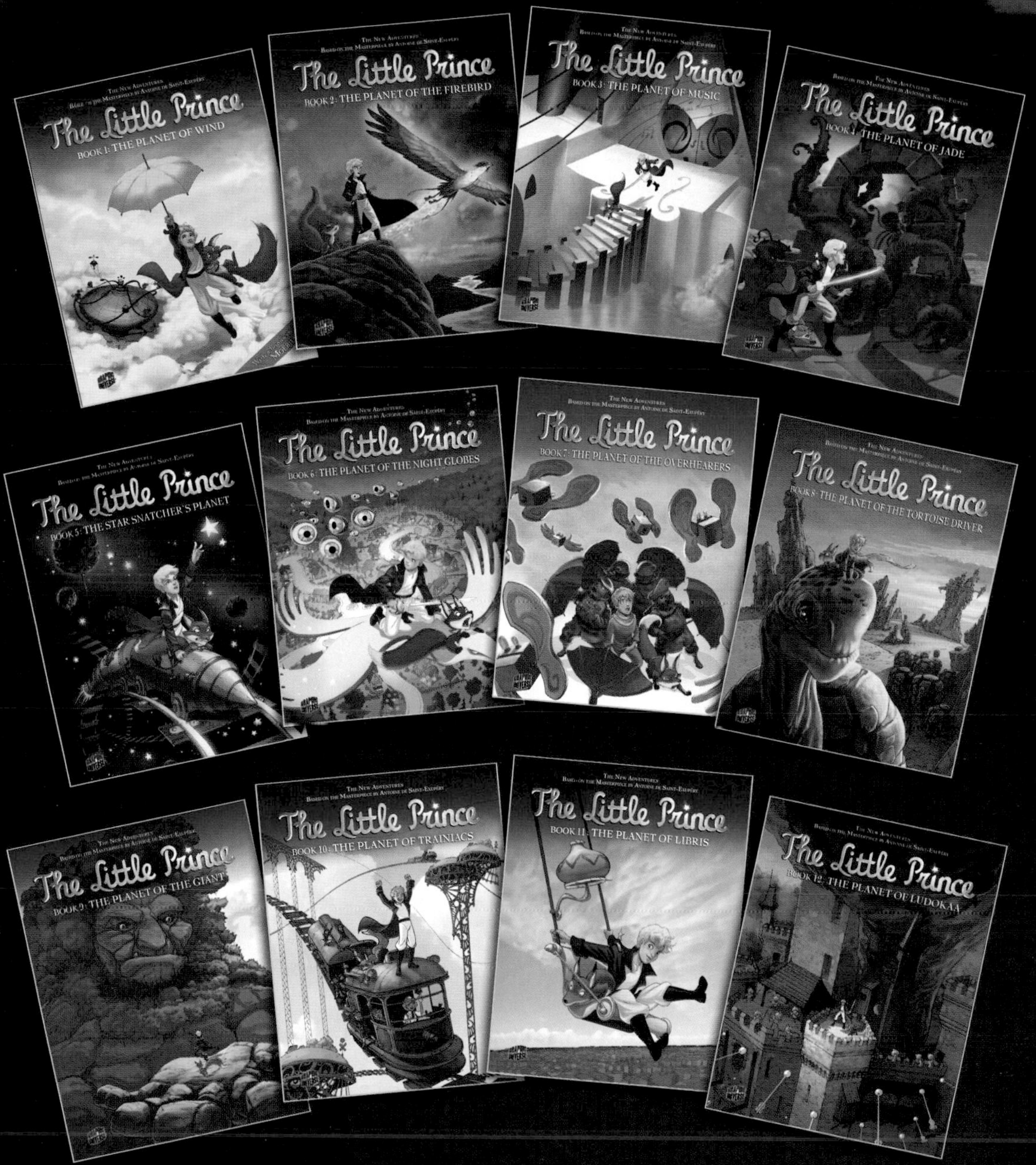
The Little Prince
Book 1: The Planet of Wind
The Little Prince
Book 2: The Planet of the Firebird
The Little Prince
Book 3: The Planet of Music
The Little Prince
Book 4: The Planet of Jade
The Little Prince
Book 5: The Star Snatcher's Planet
The Little Prince
Book 6: The Planet of the Night Globes
The Little Prince
Book 7: The Planet of the Overhearers
The Little Prince
Book 8: The Planet of the Tortoise Driver
The Little Prince
Book 9: The Planet of the Giant
The Little Prince
Book 10: The Planet of Trainiacs
The Little Prince
Book 11: The Planet of Libris
The Little Prince
Book 12: The Planet of Ludokaa

Book 1: The Planet of Wind

Book 2: The Planet of the Firebird

Book 3: The Planet of Music

Book 4: The Planet of Jade

Book 5: The Star Snatcher's Planet

Book 6: The Planet of the Night Globes

Book 7: The Planet of the Overhearers

Book 8: The Planet of the Tortoise Driver

Book 9 : The Planet of the Giant

Book 10 : The Planet of Trainiacs

Book 11 : The Planet of Libris

Book 12 : The Planet of Ludokaa

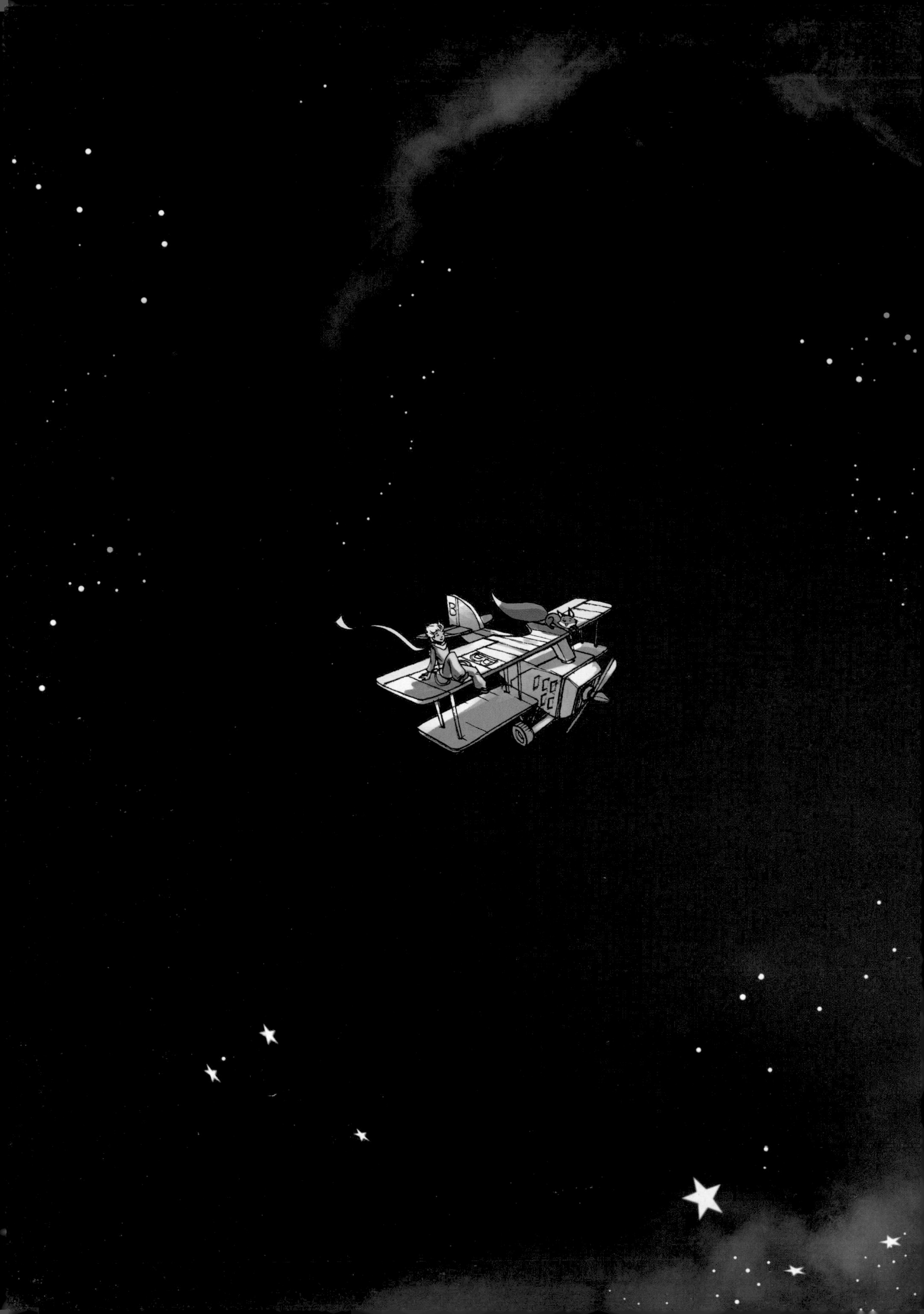